PASSION!
in Park Slope

CAROL GRAHAM

This is a work of fiction. Unless otherwise indicated, all the names, characters, businesses, places, events, and incidents in this book are either the product of the author's imagination or used in a fictitious manner. Any resemblance to actual persons, living or dead, or actual events is purely coincidental.

Copyright © 2023 Carol Graham

Cover Design by Miblart
Map Design by Lynne Moerder
Graphic on page 1 by studiogstock(Image #15446406 at VectorStock.com)

ISBN: 979-8-9887830-1-5

LCCN: 2023945889

All rights reserved, which includes the right to reproduce this book or portions thereof in any form whatsoever except as provided by the U.S. Copyright Law. For information, please address brooklynmurdermysteries@gmail.com.

Publisher's Cataloging-in-Publication (Provided by Cassidy Cataloguing Services, Inc.)
Names: Graham, Carol, 1955- author.
Title: Passion! in Park Slope / Carol Graham.
Description: [Woodstock, New York] : Quixote Publishing, [2023] | Series: Brooklyn murder mysteries ; [1]
Identifiers: ISBN: 9798988783015 (paperback) | 9798215956755 (ebook) | LCCN: 2023945889
Subjects: LCSH: Women real estate agents--New York (State)--New York--Fiction. | Detectives--New York (State)--New York--Fiction. | Brokers--New York (State)--New York--Fiction. | Murder-- Investigation--Fiction. | Park Slope (New York, N.Y.)--Fiction. | LCGFT: Cozy mysteries. | Detective and mystery fiction. | BISAC: FICTION / Mystery & Detective / Cozy / General. | FICTION / Mystery & Detective / Amateur Sleuth. | FICTION / Mystery & Detective / Women Sleuths.
Classification: LCC: PS3607.R3368 P37 2023 | DDC: 813/.6--dc23

Quixote Publishing

Table of Contents

862 Carroll Street	1
Park Place	9
6th Avenue and Dean	27
7th Avenue	39
Vanderbilt	47
7th Avenue	51
Beth Elohim	57
8th Avenue	63
The Precinct	75
5th Avenue	83
On the Cusp	91
Al Di La	95
Park Place	107
7th Avenue	111
Fort Greene, by Phone	119
7th Avenue and Berkeley	125
The Office	131
862 Carroll, Redux	139
Home	157
About Carol Graham	159

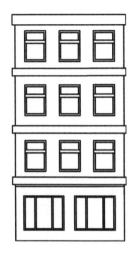

862 Carroll Street

Cara Gerard, appropriately hatted and gloved for February, pulled her silver Honda CR-V into the space beside the hydrant, a couple of feet from the curb—maybe it would look like an oh-so-temporary, just-dashing-inside-for-a-minute parking job—and told the Fishers with a wink, "I'm such a risk-taker!" as she hustled them out of the car and up the sidewalk to the stoop of the brownstone at 862 Carroll Street.

"How many tickets do you get?" the serious young husband, Dan Fisher asked.

"Oh, gosh! I quit counting!" Since becoming a realtor

in Brooklyn, just about ten years ago, she'd just called all tickets "parking" and paid them as if they were garage fees. That way, two things were accomplished: she felt that she contributed to the city that had become home to her, and she didn't squander her serenity on something beyond her control, at least regarding tickets. As usual, Cara had only limited time with these clients, and she was not going to waste any of it driving around and around looking for legal spots. Besides, she had a schedule to maintain. This parlor-level three-bedroom in the north end of Park Slope promised to be a good one, and based on the photographs, both she and the well-heeled couple who accompanied her were excited about seeing it. There were three apartments on her schedule to show them on this cold, but sunny Friday afternoon. The appointments were tight, but she was determined to get them all in. Real three-bedrooms under two million in this neighborhood, and in this school district, were not all that easy to come by. Cara felt it was a good thing she'd gotten the keys for this one, instead of having to wait for an agent to let them in. She had decided to start with this apartment, since they were going out earlier than they'd thought, instead of ending the tour with it, as originally planned, so they could allow more time for a coffee and feedback when they finished up this afternoon.

The listing broker for this brownstone apartment worked out of Cara's office and she and Cara had done a few deals together in the past, but Hannah Bauer was not one of Cara's favorite people. Hannah Bauer had been the number one agent at the Park Slope office of Corbin-Wheeler for ten years in a row. She had two assistants, was very well-known, and her success was not attributed to an easy-going personality. She was a shark—a well-dressed shark—who was extremely good at her job in a highly competitive business, in one of the most competitive markets in the country, at the biggest real estate brokerage in the city. Cara didn't mind dealing with Hannah—she had before, and would again. She had been happy enough in this case to make arrangements for showing this apartment with one of Hannah's assistants: A seemingly efficient young woman with a blandly pleasant personality and a willingness to put in the hours that a top-rated agent like Hannah Bauer required of her "team". And Hannah's definition of team, in this case, meant that she was the boss, and they were the flunkies. DeeAnn Martin had set up the appointment and left the keys for Cara in an envelope at the front desk of their busy office.

"As long as they're back by end of day, you can go anytime," she'd emailed to Cara. "I do need to have the keys back for showings on Saturday." That was not-so-subtle wording to suggest to Cara that other buyers were circling, and that she should get her clients to move quickly, though whether or not that was true was always a question. Cara acknowledged the arrangement and assured the young woman that she understood. She had always gotten along with Hannah; it didn't pay to be at odds with colleagues, particularly in the same office, but their styles were altogether different. Cara—mid-fifties and originally from Texas—had recently been called a "straight shooter" by her friend and colleague Tom Stephens. She rather liked the description. Certainly her plain spoken manner of dealing with buyers and sellers alike came from her hardscrabble upbringing in a place where pretensions were not often rewarded, and by her well-educated and unfortunately transplanted Yankee mother who did not suffer fools gladly. Cara could generally hold her own with most people. It was just Hannah's style that made her inwardly roll her eyes. For instance, Hannah often addressed other female agents as "Gorgeous" and male agents as "Handsome" when she was doing business with them. She would pass someone on the stairs and say, "Morning, Gorgeous!" without pausing for discourse of any kind, or "Hey, Handsome, when can we expect that board application?" Hannah was good-looking, somewhere in the middle of her forties, and appeared to be at the top of her game. Yes, you were "Gorgeous" or "Handsome" when the deal was on, but after the closing—which she rarely attended—you went back to being just another face in the office. Hannah Bauer was good at being Hannah Bauer.

Leading the way up the stoop, Cara inserted the key into the lock of the grandly imposing oak door of the four-story brownstone. She always held her breath when entering these stately one-hundred-year-old buildings. Locks could be sticky. She also liked to be a few steps ahead of her people so that she could flip on the first set of lights inside. She wanted a good first impression.

Turning the key easily, however, Cara pushed through both entry doors and turned to the right to the heavy walnut double door marked with the number one. Smiling and nodding over her shoulder at her clients, she started through the apartment entrance, looking for the light switch. As she turned to step aside for these buyers, to allow them an unencumbered view of the sweeping and deep parlor floor with the twelve-foot ceilings described in the listing, she realized that more than halfway back, through the double parlor of the living room, almost to the dining room, somebody—no, some bodies—were lying on the floor. And these two bodies were in the throes of very involved and very enthusiastic sex!

Cara—surprised as she was—recovered quickly, turned and practically shoved the startled Fishers back out of the door and ushered them out of the building and down to the car. They all jumped in, as Cara yanked the keys from her coat pocket, and started the engine. The three of them uttered not a word until they had pulled away from the curb, and got to the end of the block. Cara looked at her two passengers, and they, mouths still open and wordless, looked back at her. Cara shook her head. "Well, that's a first!"

The young husband in the backseat looked aghast. "Did the owners not know we were coming?"

"Dan, I don't know what to say, but I made this appointment yesterday. I am so sorry. I'll make a phone call and we'll reschedule. Meanwhile, onward and upward!"

Cara forged ahead with insight into the next listing appointment and probably babbled a bit, still feeling slightly flustered by the vision of two naked people intertwined on a beautiful oriental rug, *right there in front of God and everybody.* She'd been told by DeeAnne that the owners were away for several weeks and that it was "easy to show."

She also knew that it wasn't, as Dan Fisher was assuming, the owners that were entwined on the living room floor. She hadn't gotten a good look at the man flat on his back, but she had seen as clear as day the woman astride that man. It was the #1 Broker in Park Slope—Hannah Bauer!

The next two appointments went quickly, though including drive time and parking, they took nearly two hours. Cara tried calling and texting Hannah's assistant to no avail. Finally she left a message on Hannah's phone. "Hey, Hannah, Cara Gerard here—can you give me a quick call when you get this message? I am headed over to your listing on Carroll in about an hour, and have a quick question. Thanks!" She had her fingers crossed that those lovers had wrapped things up.

"Okay y'all—862 Carroll Street, take two!"

Cara found a "real" parking space at the end of the block. "Let's do this: I will run in first and make sure the coast is clear, and then come back and get you. How's that?" Dan and Molly Fisher nodded in agreement, and took out their cell phones to occupy themselves. They were young enough to be tech savvy, and old enough, and well-employed enough, to have the latest in electronic devices.

Cara laughed ruefully as she made her way up the sidewalk and past the stately brownstones with well-tended entries and grand fronts. Park Slope was the neighborhood that must have given the term "Brownstone Brooklyn" to the world. She knew that back in the fifties and sixties, this neighborhood had not been at its best—had been considered sketchy, even. Since sometime in the eighties, the reclaiming of these magnificent homes by the city's more upscale citizens had led to a steady climb in prices, and a neighborhood with prestige. And schools to match.

Oh, brother . . . this job! She thought back to her first entry into this apartment today. *Never dull, that's for sure.* Her next thought as she inserted the key, was that she hoped like hell that they weren't laying there still—smoking cigarettes in some kind of postcoital bliss. *Oh for god's sake—it's been two hours. Surely they are back in their own homes by now, lying to their respective spouses.* Cara knocked loudly on the apartment door anyway, just in case, and paused. It was not a scene she cared to repeat. She knocked again and gently pushed the door open.

"Hello?" She called again. "Hello?" As she walked through the well-furnished parlor toward the kitchen she noticed a shoe on the floor. "What the—" Then she saw the foot it belonged on—attached to the body splayed awkwardly half-nude and half-sitting against the cabinet below the sink. Disheveled, this person had a bright red wool scarf, twisted and rope-like, wrapped tightly around her neck—eyes open and staring but seeing nothing. Cara gasped and covered her mouth to stifle the scream she felt rising from her gut. For the second time today, she found herself caught off guard by Hannah Bauer. It was Park Slope's Broker of the Year. Dead. Dead as she could be.

Park Place

The next few hours were a nightmare. Cara's first call—to 911—was made standing on the stoop just outside the building's outer door. As soon as she hung up, she realized that her chest felt constricted to the point of gasping, and she had no idea what she had just said. The sun suddenly felt too harsh and too bright. *Breathe, Cara, breathe,* she told herself. Next, she called her managing director, Patrick Russo, and left a message on his cell phone. She thought that she should be inside with Hannah, then remembered that the Fishers were sitting in her car. She knew she could do nothing for Hannah at this point so she walked quickly towards her car as the phone rang and she heard sirens at the same instant. Glancing at her phone, she saw it was Patrick, and answered on the first ring.

"Patrick, I came into one of Hannah Bauer's listings at 862 Carroll and found her on the floor. She—she's dead. I've called the police, but I thought I should tell you too."

"Oh my God, Cara. I'm on my way."

The Fishers were still sitting in the Honda when she opened the driver side and leaned in. "Y'all, I just found the agent inside the apartment and I—I think she's dead. I've called the police. I'm going to wait on the stoop 'til they get here. I don't know what else to do. But I think you should stay put."

She slammed the car door shut, put her hand on her head to make sure her brown felt fedora stayed securely atop her head, and ran up the sidewalk. Sitting at the top of the stoop, she put her head in her hands and tried to think. Her thoughts were jumbled, but she knew she had to slow down and be calm. Hannah Bauer was dead, and Cara may have been the last person other than the man she'd been having sex with, and of course the murderer, to see her alive. Were the other two one and the same person?

When the uniformed officers arrived, Cara took them inside the apartment and then they directed her back to the stoop. More police arrived and began to cordon off the area around 862—sidewalk and street. Moments in, a dark gray SUV pulled up and a tall, good-looking man, sixtyish with close-cropped gray hair, a serious expression, and a dark brown leather jacket stepped out, took in the scene with a slow sweep, and stopped when he got to the stoop and Cara. He strode the few paces towards her and looked up. "Are you Cara Gerard? Did you call this in?"

"Yes, I am. I did."

"I'm Detective Driscoll, NYPD." He flashed a badge. "Can you come with me?"

Cara felt instantly relieved. This was a man used to being in charge. Driscoll's voice was calm and his manner reassuring. He gestured her to his car and opened the passenger door for her.

"Ms. Gerard, I'm going inside for a few minutes. Can you wait here? I need to ask some questions and will need a statement, but I need to view the scene."

"Yes, of course."

Cara texted the Fishers to let them know what was happening. They would no doubt be getting antsy. When Detective Driscoll returned to the car, he asked, "Are you okay?"

"I guess so. Detective Driscoll, my clients that I brought here to show this apartment to, are in my car at the end of the block. They waited in the car for me to check out the apartment, and I found Hannah before they came in, but they're still here. They have kids to pick up, so if you could talk to them first, I can wait."

"They didn't enter the apartment?"

"No, well—not this time. We were here earlier today. They didn't come in with me just now, when I found Hannah. It's Dan and Molly Fisher. And my car is the silver CR-V at the end of the block on this side."

"Okay." He walked down to talk to the Fishers and was back in short order. "They're walking home. Now, Ms. Gerard, can you tell me what happened? Start at the beginning." Cara took a breath, and recounted her afternoon starting with the sex scene she'd walked in on.

Driscoll faced her, listening carefully, with no interruptions until she stopped talking. "Can your other appointments today be verified?"

"Yes. The other appointments were with other agents. And, of course, the Fishers. Detective Driscoll, the scarf around her neck was twisted and looked really tight. Is that what killed her? Someone strangled her?"

"Well, it looks that way, but we'll have to wait for the coroner's report, so please don't spread that around."

He looked out the window, thinking. "Did you know the deceased well? She gave you keys for this apartment, instead of arranging to be here with you? Is that common practice?"

"Well, only sometimes. The owners are away, apparently, and I have done other deals with Hannah. I mean, she knows me, and knows I'm reliable, and will be careful about locking up and such. Knew me. Actually I made these arrangements with her assistant, though. DeeAnne Martin."

"Okay. And you didn't recognize the man she was with earlier? You don't think it was her husband?"

"I don't think so. I've never met her husband, but I've seen him on her Facebook posts. This guy today was blond, I think, and younger, maybe. But that's an after-the-fact impression. I am not sure why I'm saying that even. I didn't get a good look at his face, or any other part of him. As I said, I got out of there as quickly as I could. I didn't want the Fishers to see that. I didn't want to see it myself."

"Did you notice any clothing or anything else that might help us?"

Cara thought for a minute, and shook her head. "No."

"Ms. Gerard, I'm going to ask you to humor me. Close your eyes for a minute, please. And see if you can visualize coming in that door for the first time, today."

Cara hesitated, then did as she was asked.

"Can you see it? Are you there?"

She nodded.

"What do you see?"

"There's a coat, I think, on the sofa, just inside the living room. Camel-colored, maybe."

"Anything else? Something out of place?"

Cara opened her eyes. "Other than the people having sex on the floor? No. I'd never been in that apartment before, so I wouldn't know if something was out of place or not."

Detective Driscoll nodded. "Okay. So you knew the deceased. Was she a friend?"

"No, I wouldn't say that. We worked in the same office for several years, and I've done a couple of deals with her, but we've never even had coffee."

"Did she have friends in your office?"

"Detective Driscoll, Hannah Bauer was a very successful agent. She's been the top broker in our office for years. It's a competitive business. I don't think many of us are friends, really. But Hannah . . . she was really successful and really competitive. I think a lot of the agents were probably slightly jealous of her. I don't know if anybody really liked her. Other than Laura Simonson. My understanding is that they were friends. I think Hannah brought Laura into the business. And they may have kids the same age. I'm not really sure. Neither one of them is my friend, so that's a vague impression, not a fact."

"I see. Have you ever heard anyone say anything to her, or about her, that seemed more than just 'slightly' jealous?"

"I have never heard anyone say they hated her guts or wished she was dead, if that's what you are asking. She often stepped on people's toes, but in this business, it happens."

"Okay, thank you, Ms. Gerard. Would you come by the station tomorrow and make a formal statement? Anytime between eleven and two would be best."

"Yes, I can do that. I'll see you at eleven."

"And if you think of anything else, this evening, here's my card."

Cara climbed out of Detective Driscoll's car and started walking to her own. She spotted Patrick Russo almost running up the sidewalk and she stopped to have a word with him. After quickly giving him the short version, she realized she was exhausted. She opened her car door, climbed in, and took a breath. Then she texted the Fishers to say she would check in the next day, and apologized for the way the day turned out. Cara was not sure why she was apologizing, but felt the need to say something. It was maybe her Southern-girl mentality kicking in, or maybe not. She was sorry the afternoon had ended so horribly. Hannah Bauer was dead. *Unbelievable.*

She had lost people close to her in her life. Her father had died when she was ten, and her ex-husband had died piloting his Piper Cherokee in New Mexico, shortly after their divorce. Cara's dear friend Terra, a close friend since college, had died five years before from injuries sustained in a car crash. All that loss had been so hard, and Cara was no stranger to the idea of death, but if she was reading this afternoon's events correctly, Hannah's death was no accident, or medical fluke. Hannah Bauer had been murdered. Cara knew that this woman was not well liked. Disliked, in fact, by some. But who could have hated her enough to kill her?

Cara Gerard was an intelligent woman. And she'd seen things. She'd grown up in Texas: her redneck father/Yankee mother upbringing was an odd but useful combination of Southern Belle and pull-yourself-up-by-your-bootstraps. Though her father had died when she was in the fourth grade, she'd been his favorite and thus appreciated men, and had in fact, married three, but always found a reason to be on her own. She was stubborn and a hard worker and certainly had a mind of her own. Her mother—a cold, well-educated teetotaler from Boston—was probably responsible for that side of her. Her father—a charmer who drank himself to death when he was forty-nine—gave her another set of characteristics.

Alcohol had not seemed like a problem to Cara until her brother, a divorced father of two, and just a few years older than she was, had died behind the wheel of his Toyota pickup, drunk on a Thursday afternoon outside Lubbock. Another loss. Though they had not been as close as they once were, Cara loved him, and realized how similar their involvement with alcohol had been. It had no longer been a casual relationship, but a way of life for her that clearly—from the loss of both her father and brother—seemed destined to end, and end badly. Towards the end of her last marriage (to the husband she had really wanted to keep) she had put down the drink, found the twelve-step recovery group, and worked hard to stay sober. Now in her mid-fifties, she was sober nearly twenty years and had been a New Yorker—born-again New Yorker, she liked to say—for ten of those years, and a realtor for almost as long.

Cara liked her life. New York City, and Brooklyn in particular, suited her well. She liked the anonymity available to her and the excitement and diversity of the city, but figured out early on that the neighborhoods in this metropolitan area of eight million people, were really like small towns. The dry cleaners, the grocery, the pharmacy, and the delis in the neighborhood were places where she knew people. And they knew her. The bank manager at the branch across from her office always greeted her by name. Cara often ran into people on the street that she knew, or had helped find a home. Schezuan Delight always included a small container of sweet and sour sauce when she ordered a combination platter for takeout, because Mrs. Wong knew without asking she liked it with her egg roll. Cara had found a comfortable, though not necessarily always easy, place in the world for herself when she found Brooklyn, and Park Slope. It was beautiful and looked to her the way New York did in the movies. She had left the Southwest behind her, and rarely looked back, though her Texas twang hadn't been replaced by a Brooklyn accent, by any means. New Yorkers often asked her where she was from. She liked to say, "South Brooklyn" just to catch them off guard for a moment, before she would chuckle and say, "No, kidding. I'm from Texas." She had often thought to herself that people here on the East Coast heard her drawl, and slowed their own speech to match it, and sometimes spoke a little louder, like maybe she was slightly deaf, or maybe a little slow-witted. If they thought that, however, they would be mistaken. And she'd straighten them out on that, one way or the other. She was not above using that slight dip in someone's defenses, in a negotiation. If they sold her short, based on her twang, they'd eventually learn they had been in error. She didn't have the connections of someone like Hannah Bauer, and hadn't started in the real estate business early enough in her life to create the longevity that surely contributed to the success of Park Slope's broker of the year. Cara was not a shark, but she had her own brand of shrewdness, was a good listener, had a good eye, and was persistent. She'd been fairly successful since she had begun in real estate and every year had been better than the last. Cara was satisfied with this career path, and enjoyed most of the time she spent at it. That is, until today. Finding a colleague, even one she didn't like all that much, dead, was more than upsetting. Cara felt off-kilter, sad, and more than anything, angry. Hannah Bauer may not have been a peach to deal with, but Cara had a certain amount of respect for her. She didn't deserve to end up like that.

She pushed open the door to her building on Park Place, said hello to the part-time doorman, and reached for the keys in her pocket. *Damn!* She had forgotten to return the keys to 862 Carroll to the office. *Well, it probably doesn't matter now*, she thought. She unlocked her door, hung her coat in the tiny front closet, and placed her pencil-rimmed fedora on an empty spot on the rack near the door.

Cara was a wearer of hats. She had been since her high school days in her small West Texas hometown that had, in her mind then, been flat and rather dull and completely devoid of anything interesting, and certainly without style. At first, she wore floppy straw ones in the summer, and then branched out to quirky knit or leather styles to suit the so-called seasons. West Texas weather didn't usually call for radical clothing changes, so she created her own seasonal fashion choices. One of the millinery styles she never included back in the beginning was the Western or as they were referred to there, cowboy hats. She had acquired a taste for that particular headgear the further she got from her small-town West Texas roots and as she got older and lived in different places, she found she liked them more and more. Currently there were three in her collection: two Stetsons and a Borsalino. It also included almost every genre of lid that she felt comfortable wearing: Bowler, berets, beanies, Panama, fedoras, and even a couple of baseball caps. She glanced into the mirror hanging in the entry. Her usual quick grin was nowhere to be found today. Her light auburn hair was thick and wavy, and she wore it long, just below her shoulders. Left to its own devices, it was a bit unruly. Cara called it "big hair". Once she'd hit fifty, it began to get lighter and lighter, and if it kept going that way, she guessed she would be strawberry blonde like her older sister. She was aware it was her best feature, though she never wanted to be thought vain about it. It may have been the very reason she wore hats—to quiet it. Tall and curvy, she was most comfortable in jeans, and dressed them up with a variety of jackets, vests and blazers. And of course, hats. Hats had, over the years, become her signature look. And these days the number of hats in her collection had grown to a number big enough to cover almost one whole wall of the foyer in her small New York apartment. Most of them hung on wooden knobs, or interesting hooks, but some were perched on glass or carved wood or even plastic heads on shelves. They had become an art installation. An interactive art installation.

She headed for the kitchen, putting water on to boil and took down her favorite cup for tea. It was the one she bought in London last year when she and her friend Mary O'Brien had gone to see Eric Clapton's birthday concert at the Royal Albert Hall. It was just the right size for tea, and covered in beautiful red poppies. Red was Cara's favorite color. She had spotted the cup in a window on Portobello Road, and bought it along with the tiny little creamer that matched. She enjoyed the ritual of tea, the time involved in the preparation, and today she wanted the comfort of something warm and delicious and beautiful to take the ugliness out of the afternoon's events. She opened the Harney and Sons tin and withdrew a sachet of Earl Grey. If anything could help her feel calmer it was this: a well-brewed cup of tea and a phone call to Mary.

Mary O'Brien was several years older than Cara, and very lean and athletic. A brunette with an easy-care pageboy, she moved gracefully thru the world, attentive and self-aware. She'd always been a beauty, conscientious of her diet, and had a personal trainer that she worked out with twice a week. She had had a Catholic school upbringing in Scarsdale, and had come to Brooklyn, after a graduate degree at Yale. Mary was smart and thoughtful. Cara took her phone out of her bag and called her friend who answered right away, and with the same greeting she always used when Cara called her at the end of the day. "Hey, there, how was real estate?"

"Oh, gosh, Mary! The most awful thing happened! I was showing an apartment and I walked in and found the listing agent on the floor, dead. It looked like she'd been strangled. I still can't believe it!"

"My God! Was it someone you knew? What did you do?"

"Well, I called the police. But that's not all . . ." Cara took a sip of tea and related the whole afternoon's events, from start to finish. There was silence on the other end of the phone.

"Are you still there?" Cara asked.

"Yeah . . . I just don't know what to say."

"Me neither."

"Did you see who the guy was?"

"No, not really. I have an image of a blond guy, but I'm not sure how accurate that is. I turned away and bolted as soon as I realized what was happening. I didn't want the Fishers to see that."

"Oh, God, no! That's awful!"

"I know! I have to go to the police station tomorrow to make a formal statement."

"At the one on 6th?"

"Yeah. I told my story to the detective who showed up today, but I guess they want to hear it again."

"So who do you think did it?"

"Gosh, I don't know. I've been pondering that all afternoon. The guy she was doing on the oriental rug? Her husband who found out about the guy she was doing on the oriental rug? Or 95 percent of the real estate agents in Brooklyn who couldn't stand her?"

"Is that true? She was not well-liked?"

"Well, you've heard me talk about her before. Hannah Bauer. She's a piece of work. I'm sure she had friends. Just nobody I know."

"Oh . . ."

Cara hung up after talking to Mary for as long as her tea lasted, and sat thinking about Hannah Bauer. She knew Hannah had a husband and a teenage daughter. Surely she had friends. *Maybe*, Cara thought, *I'm not giving her enough credit. Still, Hannah had one person angry enough in her life to want her dead. Unless it was random. But that makes no sense.*

Cara picked up her phone and called Tom Stephens. Tom and his partner, Jim Alcott, were Corbin-Wheeler agents as well as good friends to Cara. She had often thought that she wouldn't have been doing this job as long as she had without them. Tom, Jim, and Cara relied on each other for many things. Tom and Jim were partners in life as well as in their real estate business, and Cara often found herself the deciding vote in a tied-up real estate decision between the two men. And they, in turn, gave well-thought-out opinions and insight when she found herself in a dilemma. They also covered for each other when time away was needed. The three friends sat side by side in the Park Slope office and in the fast-paced, often stressful world of New York City real estate, they counted on each other for sage counsel and a sense of humor when the going got tough. The two men were good brokers. They were also funny, good-looking and smart.

Tom and Jim had both been in the business, and in the Park Slope office, for a few years longer than Cara, and of course, knew Hannah Bauer.

"Hey, honey, how did it go today? See anything worth selling?" Tom had taken the day off, and sounded well-rested.

"Jesus, Tom, you are not going to believe what's happened. Is Jim around? Y'all put me on speaker."

When Jim and Tom had heard the whole story, there was silence on both ends of the phone. Jim was the first one to speak.

"My God, how horrible. What do you think, angry husband or angry real estate broker?"

"I'm wondering. It seems impossible either way. Have you ever met her husband?"

"Nope. But really—crime of passion, right? It happens every day in America. And remember last year when the rumor mill said that Hannah was getting a divorce? I heard he moved out for a while, but I guess it never came to be."

"Well, there are also probably more than a few agents who have been burned by her methods," Tom said. "We heard Laura Simonson yelling over her phone in the kitchen at the office a couple days ago, and I am pretty sure it was at Hannah."

"Really? I thought they were friends."

"Funny—that's exactly what Laura said. Or shouted, actually."

"Could you tell what she was upset about?" Cara asked.

"No, not really. We were trying too hard to pretend it wasn't happening. I did hear her say at one point, 'how long have you been keeping this from me?' and then 'you are such an effing liar!'"

"She said 'effing?'"

"No, I said effing. She said the real word."

Tom interjected, "That's when I put on my earphones. I couldn't believe she was screaming at someone in the office. I do think it was Hannah, too, though. I am not sure exactly why. She must've said 'Hannah' at some point though, 'cause we both thought that she was getting into it with Hannah."

"Hmmm."

"Well, she'll never have to worry about being lied to by Hannah again. I know that'll be a relief." Jim said.

"Jim!" Tom exclaimed.

"Oh, I'm just kidding. You know that. It's horrible, of course."

"You are the worst!" Cara said, but couldn't help smiling, as she shook her head.

"I can't help it."

"Well, try!" Tom said. "Cara, are you okay? That must have been traumatic to walk in and find her like that."

"It was pretty awful. I am just glad I had the Fishers sit in the car. After seeing them having sex, I don't know if Molly Fisher could have recovered from finding her like that. I am not sure I can either." Cara wondered what was happening at the Bauer home, speaking of awful. That poor Detective Driscoll. It had to be hard telling a husband and a daughter that their wife and mother had been murdered. *Well, unless Benjamin Bauer did it.* As Jim pointed out, it wouldn't be the first time a husband was the murderer.

Saying goodbye to her friends, Cara realized she hadn't checked her texts in hours. When she looked at them, she froze. There was one from Hannah Bauer, and it was apparently in response to the ones that Cara had left earlier in the afternoon, about an hour after the first visit to the apartment. *Hey, Gorgeous! Got your message. Thought you were coming tomorrow (Sat) but okay. Come anytime after about 3:00. Let's sell it!*

Oh, gosh. Another "last thing" from Hannah. Cara reached for Detective Driscoll's card and dialed his number. She wanted him to know about this text and that it was sent at 2:03. Since she and the Fishers had returned to Carroll Street about 3:15, it indicated about a one hour window for someone to kill Hannah. It felt really creepy. She was glad it was a text and not a voice mail. It would have been too much to hear Hannah's voice. She left a voicemail for the detective, when he didn't pick up, and confirmed she would be at the station tomorrow by 11:00.

Cara immediately ordered Shrimp Pad Thai and Crab Rangoon from the Thai place on 7th Avenue. Asian comfort food. That's what she needed right now. No way was she up for cooking herself something for dinner tonight. This day felt like it had been a week. And tomorrow she was going to have to live through the whole thing again, when she made a statement at the police station. As her Grandfather Pop Wesson, a cowboy Cara had been particularly close to used to say: she felt like she had been "rode hard and put away wet." Sometimes his old rodeo expressions came to her, and were a comfort. Today, she would take all the comfort she could get.

6th Avenue and Dean

Cara walked into the police station on 6th Avenue and Dean the next morning, bundled up in her black wool parka and a navy blue Greek fisherman's cap. She approached the officer at the front desk. It was a very busy place, with uniformed officers coming and going, sometimes with people in handcuffs, calling out to one another, or working at desks, answering phones and typing. As soon as she asked for Detective Driscoll, she was directed up the stairs to the office at the end of the hall.

Driscoll met her at his door and offered her coffee.

"No thanks. I'm all coffee'd up."

"It's not really worth drinking, anyway, though I do, I'm afraid," he said sitting behind a desk covered with papers and Styrofoam cups, and manila folders with circular coffee stains from those Styrofoam cups. He was broad-shouldered and tall, and Cara thought to herself, *He needs a bigger desk.* "Ms. Gerard, I'm going to get my sergeant in here to record your statement and take notes, if that's okay with you. I don't want to miss anything. Also—thanks for letting me know about the text message."

"That's fine. I don't know that I have thought of anything new to add, but I feel like I was so rattled yesterday, I'm not sure of what I said, so it will probably be good for me to go through it again."

"Most people are like that. It's not an easy situation to be in." *He has sad eyes*, Cara thought, *but clear and direct. He's seen some hard things.*

"We also would like to get your finger prints so we can eliminate those from any others. Won't take long, and we'll have you on your way." He spoke into the phone on his desk, and a moment later an officer walked in with an iPad and a notebook, and sat down in another chair near Cara.

"Ms. Gerard, Officer Rodriguez." Cara nodded and settled in. She reached into her bag for a bottle of water, and took a big swallow. Driscoll cleared his throat and picked up a pen from his desk.

"Now Ms. Gerard—"

"Please—call me Cara."

"Okay, Cara. Yesterday you indicated that Ms. Bauer was not well-liked. Do you know anyone who had had a really bad experience with her recently, or actively spoke ill of her?"

"You know, Detective Driscoll, I feel bad about saying

that. I have done business with a great many people in real estate, within our company and others, of course, and well, you just can't like everyone. Not everyone likes me, either, I'm certain of that. She, as I said, was extremely successful, and rather arrogant, but I could say that about many others. She was just not always easy to take. I've heard her give her assistants grief, in the office, a couple of times over the years, and she went thru a few of them, but it worries me to suggest any of these things as being worthy of this kind of violence."

"I understand, Cara. I am not trying to get you to say more that you can. But someone was angry enough to take her life from her, and it's my job to figure out who did that. We'll be questioning agents in your office as well as others, of course. If you can think of anything that you think might help us, I would sure appreciate your insight. Anything at all."

"Well, Detective Driscoll, I heard through the grapevine, that Laura Simonson was yelling at someone over her phone a couple of days ago, and the assumption was that it was Hannah. I don't know if that is true or not, I didn't hear that conversation myself, and I sure don't want to cause trouble for Laura, but that's what I heard." Detective Driscoll made a note on a pad in front of him.

"I understand. Now if you could start from the top and tell me about your afternoon yesterday, we'll listen and take some notes. Take your time." He nodded to Rodriguez. "Rick . . ."

Cara went thru the details as she remembered them, slowly and with great care, with Driscoll interrupting only a couple of times with questions. He also asked for the names of the other agents whose listings she had shown to the Fishers, and the specific times for everything. She referred to the calendar on her phone to verify times. Cara assumed that the detective was verifying her own alibi, as she told her story. She was, after all, first on the scene. She had seen enough TV crime drama to recognize the process.

"Okay, Cara, thanks. We'll be talking to a lot of your colleagues, and if you could say as little about this as possible, we'd appreciate it. I know that some talk will be inevitable, and word will certainly get around, but until we find the person who did this, just try to keep the details to yourself, if you don't mind. And if anything comes to your attention that you think beneficial, please call me."

"I will." Cara hesitated as she gathered her coat and bag. "Detective Driscoll, I feel a bit awkward, but I don't know who else to talk about this with."

"What is it?"

"Well, while I don't know Hannah's husband, I was a colleague of hers and have known her for almost ten years. If she had died under more normal circumstances, I would pay a visit to her family, or send flowers or something, but especially since I was the last person to see her, maybe, or because I found her like that, I don't know just how to approach them. I am wondering what they were told about the circumstances just before she died. I am worried if Ben Bauer knows that I found her, that he will ask me about it, and I don't know what to say."

"I understand. Mr. Bauer was told the truth about both

your visits. That is all I can say. And as for your actions, I think you should do what feels right to you, Cara. If Mr. Bauer questions you, you can refer him to me. Tell him you said everything you had to say to me."

"Okay, thank you." Officer Rodriguez led Cara downstairs and up to a window where another officer inked her fingertips and rolled her prints on a pad. Once she washed up, she headed out the door.

It was a fifteen-minute walk to the Corbin-Wheeler office on 7th Avenue, and one that Cara always enjoyed, no matter the season. Winter was her favorite time of year—she'd spent many years skiing the mountains of New Mexico and Colorado—and this particular day was what she always categorized as a "Santa Fe day". It was cold and sharp and the sun was squintably bright. Her favorite weather. Winter in the city was definitely different from the mountains in New Mexico, but the arrival of snow always made her skier's heart beat fast. There hadn't been any since mid-January, but she was ever-hopeful. While its beauty didn't last as long in Brooklyn as it did around Santa Fe—more people, more cars, more soot—she still loved it. Though her mind was filled with thoughts of Hannah Bauer and who could have "taken her life from her" as Detective Driscoll put it, she felt good to be outside and moving. She headed to work wondering if word had gotten around the office of Hannah's death. She couldn't imagine that it hadn't. If Park Slope was like a small town, Corbin-Wheeler was a subset of that. Detective Driscoll would, no doubt, be around at some point to speak with agents who knew her, and she knew that he had spoken with her boss, Patrick, yesterday. Cara felt sure that if everyone hadn't heard about Hannah, they certainly soon would.

Walking up 7th Avenue to the office, Cara glanced at the news stand outside the deli on Berkeley Place. *The Daily News* headline shouted halfway down its front page: PARK SLOPE REALTOR MURDERED! *Oh, no!* She grabbed the paper and went inside and threw a dollar on the counter. Outside she stood in the sunshine and scanned the article. *Prominent Brooklyn broker found murdered yada yada yada, police following leads.* Cara folded the paper under her arm and continued on her way. *Okay. Well, that's that. No doubt it'll be the talk of the office now.*

As she walked she texted Patrick to set up a time to meet. She wanted to talk to him about the day before, along with the words of caution from Detective Driscoll. She wondered if there would be services, and how Corbin-Wheeler would participate. Hannah had worked for the company a long time. And she was a star.

Patrick waved her into his office as she walked by the glass cubicle.

"How are you?"

"All right. Did you talk with Detective Driscoll? Is that why you're here on a Saturday? And did you see this?" Cara handed him the Daily News.

"Yes. There are police upstairs going through Hannah's desk. Getting stuff off her computer. Hell of a thing. I wanted to be here when people in the office start hearing about it. I'm calling an office-wide meeting for tomorrow morning to make an announcement. I'm sure most of the agents will have heard by then, but since Saturday is usually a little drowsy, as far as office activity, they may not, if they don't read the Daily News. I didn't want our weekend receptionist to handle things by herself. I still can't believe it. I am sorry you found her. If you want to talk about it, I'm here."

"Well, Driscoll asked me not to . . . but thanks."

"Right—murder. It seems unimaginable."

"I know. Anyway—is her family going to let us know about services and burial and such? I'm not sure what to do, exactly, because I don't know her husband. I met her daughter once, but it was a few years ago. She was still a little girl, really. She must be fifteen or sixteen now."

"Yeah, something like that. I'll be speaking with the higher ups about the services. I'm sure we'll be notified when something is set up. I'll get back to you, but if you hear something first, let me know, will you?"

"Will do." Cara went upstairs to her desk and glanced over to the big floor-to-ceiling windows that overlooked 7th Avenue, where Hannah and her two assistants had their desks. It was the plum spot, for sure, but the view was simply the commercial avenue in Park Slope. Still, Hannah had had first choice, no doubt, when the office had expanded up from the street level and taken over the space formerly filled by a lackluster pizza joint. She'd picked the big front windows. Spiteful colleagues said it was so she could continue to look down on everybody. Maybe it was. Cara wondered just how many enemies Hannah Bauer had made in her climb to the top. Or was there an easier answer—and her murder the result of a jealous husband? *More will be revealed*, she thought, as she observed two policeman going through Hannah's desk drawers.

After checking in on the Fishers and letting them know that there were two open houses on Sunday that they might want to see on their own, Cara finished up some research for a couple of different buyers that she'd been working with for several months. They both wanted one-bedrooms in perfect locations in elevator buildings, with private outdoor space, and they didn't want to pay an arm and a leg. *Well, probably not going to happen.* She knew, and her buyers were coming to know, that an arm and a leg was exactly how much such apartments cost. Something had to give, if one wanted to keep the price down. Cara always asked buyers that she was working with to make a list of their top five requirements for the apartment of their dreams. She then told them that while she would look for all those wants, her experience told her that usually compromises had to be made. It made her think of a time when she was a little girl in West Texas. She'd gone with her daddy to a mechanic's shop, where he had taken the family car for some minor repairs. It was the site of a former gas station, with a couple of bays and a small, dingy front "office", with hand-written signs taped to the walls noting prices and services offered, alongside posters of scantily-clad women sitting on the hoods of cars, promoting motor oil. There was one sign that read, "Repairs done FAST, CHEAP, RIGHT. Pick TWO!" Her dad had chuckled when she'd asked about that, but had sat down and explained the philosophy that the car mechanics were trying to get across.

She'd understood it then, and she understood it now. Sometimes she wished she had an equivalent sentiment for real estate to hang above her desk. At any rate, it was part of her job to help her buyers find the balance in the location, amenities, and price that was reality in New York City.

Cara returned emails, sent notices for open houses, including her own, and generally tied up loose ends before pulling on her parka, throwing her satchel over her shoulder, cross-body style, donning her cap and heading out the door. She was planning to take the slightly longer route home, along Prospect Park. The sunshine along with the cold crisp air, and some low-level exercise would be good for her soul. And she wanted time to think. Walking between the elegant turn-of-the-century limestone townhouses, and the impressive and vast design of the Park was exhilarating to the Texas-girl mentality that she brought to daily living in the city. It just never got old. Each building, she felt, had been built to stand for as long as there was a city. It was, in every way, unlike the flat one-story buildings she'd grown up with in West Texas: low-built to the ground and plain, to withstand the wind and harsh constancy of the sun, and not a big loss if they didn't.

Outside the waist-high walls enclosing the Park, old-fashioned wooden and iron benches were dotted intermittently, facing the street, for pedestrians to pause and rest, on the wide sidewalk that stretched from the majestic Grand Army Plaza to the south end at 15th Street. The benches were mostly empty on this chilly afternoon, though the one almost to the circle of Grand Army Plaza was occupied with one person on each end. She was approaching from the opposite side of the street. One of the men had his bike leaned up against the wall behind them, and the other—pudgy and wearing a tie and a trench coat—sat on the edge of the bench, furthest away. They didn't appear to be in conversation, or together at all, she thought, so why occupy the same bench? There were plenty of empty seats along the walkway. As she got nearer, she thought the bicyclist looked familiar. *Was that Ben Bauer?!* His round black glasses and spiked white hair made for a distinctive look, and though she'd never met him, she recognized him from Hannah's Facebook postings, most recently from a trip they'd apparently taken to the Mayan Riviera. The closer she got, the surer she was. *That's Ben Bauer!* Cara had no idea who the other man was. A friend of Ben's, maybe, offering condolences? She hoped Hannah's husband had someone to turn to in his grief.

As she was about to cross the street and pass the two men, Ben Bauer stood and said to the other man, angrily, "Give it a rest!" and reached for his bike, threw his leg over the frame and rode away. Though she was halfway through the crosswalk, she heard him clearly. She kept walking and because of her sunglasses, she could turn her head away slightly and still keep her eyes on the remaining man. He was looking straight ahead at the building on the corner. Cara kept walking, and a few steps further, she looked back over her shoulder and saw the guy do something very strange. He had a piece of paper, or a napkin, maybe, in his hand, and was tearing it into strips. Cara watched him put it in his mouth and chew, one piece at a time. She slowed her gait slightly, and kept walking, glancing back again. He swallowed the last piece, got up, and walked in the opposite direction. She frowned. *What was that about?* Her head was spinning with the weird image, and she wondered what could possibly be the reason for such bizarre behavior. Certainly this meeting had been clandestine. Who was that man and what did he need to hide so completely? And just twenty-four hours after Hannah's death. And what part did Ben Bauer play in that?

She shook her head. *Oh, brother.* Cara picked up her pace and crossed under the huge Grand Army arch. She wanted to get home and have a cup of tea. She was glad she would be going to an AA meeting later. It would be good to get out of her own head for a bit, hear what other people were dealing with, and how they applied spiritual principles to real life. The Twelve Steps for staying sober were also guides to living life outside the meetings. This was all very disturbing, and she could use a big dose of down-to-earth recovery.

7th Avenue

Sunday morning's office meeting, set up by Patrick to make a general announcement regarding Hannah Bauer's death, was extremely well-attended. A couple of the big guns from the head office in Manhattan were there, as well as Detective Driscoll, and Patrick requested that everyone cooperate fully with the police. Cara wondered if she should tell the detective about the paper-eating from yesterday. Tell him what? *That a guy I don't know ate a napkin?* It sounded absurd. Driscoll, for his part, introduced himself, and let it be known that several leads were being investigated, and most likely, all the Park Slope agents would be questioned sometime in the next few days. Cara, in the corner by the Carroll Street windows, watched the faces of her colleagues from under the brim of her soft grey-colored Trilby, as Patrick told them about Hannah's death, to see if she could pick out anyone who looked guilty. Mostly they looked shocked. Very few looked like they were grieving. But then, Cara realized that she really knew so few of these people well at all. People she saw every day at the office were not necessarily people she could call friends. Most of them were strangers to her, except for their bios posted on the Corbin-Wheeler website, or the last deal they'd done with her. There were fifty or sixty agents in this office alone, plus other offices in Brooklyn. Add that to the six offices in Manhattan, and it made for a long list of "co-workers". There was no time in life to get to know that many colleagues, but Cara had met a great many in the decade she'd been in this business, and done deals with quite a few. Other than Laura Simonson, Cara had no idea at all who might have really known and liked Hannah. Or who couldn't stand her. She just knew that agents in general were not that kind towards the top broker in the office. At least, behind her back.

After the meeting ended, everyone lingered a bit, curious as to the details that had not been included in the announcement. Sundays were the traditional day for open houses in Brooklyn, and most of the agents would be working outside of the office later in the day, but now they were loitering around Patrick's office and in the kitchen near the Nespresso machine trying to find out if anyone had more info than Patrick and the police. Cara headed up to her desk to get ready for her own open house on 6th Avenue. She was hoping she wouldn't have to talk about

Hannah's death. Patrick hadn't mentioned her role in Friday afternoon's discovery. That was fine by Cara.

She was staring at the printer waiting for copies of the floor plans of her listing, when Laura Simonson came around the corner. The movement caught Cara's attention, and she looked up to see Laura bearing down on her with a purpose. Laura was a tall, attractive woman with a year-round tan, and today, was decked out in high-waisted distressed jeans with perfectly placed holes at the knees, Stuart Weitzman ankle boots, a sheepskin bomber jacket, and a Kate Spade bag on her shoulder. Laura was the star of her own movie. From her six-hundred-dollar haircuts from Ruscha's on the Lower East Side to the au courant shoes on her feet, her "outsides" were carefully managed to exude what she considered herself to be on the inside: ageless, ever-desirable in any situation, and enviable. Laura seemed to have decided sometime in her past, after having dropped out of college and moving to New York City, that the role of ingenue would always be hers. No matter what. She strode directly up to Cara, and threw her arms around Cara's shoulders. Her eyes were puffy from crying, and mascara had left black smudges down both cheeks. She began talking mid-hug, and when she did, the tears started flowing again. Though she was in her mid-forties and originally from somewhere in the Midwest, she spoke as though she were a teenager from Southern California—her voice high and somewhat childlike, with every other sentence peppered with "like" and ending as if it were a question.

"I heard you, like, found her? Like, oh my God? I can't, like, believe it? Oh my God!"

Cara patted Laura's back and gently extracted herself from Laura's embrace. Her entrance had attracted the attention of the other agents from the kitchen and a small crowd was starting to gather.

Cara took Laura's arm, grabbed her own bag and coat from her chair, and moved Laura toward the stairs and down. "Let's go have some coffee. We need to get out of here."

Laura nodded and followed her out onto the street. Cara headed for the crepe shop up the block. It was small, but too new in the neighborhood to be crowded. Park Slope on a Sunday morning was going to be slim pickings for privacy in a breakfast place, but this would have to do. Cara wanted to speak to Laura, and the office wasn't going to work at all.

She ordered two lattes, and sat down with Laura at a small bistro table in the corner. Laura pulled herself together, and blew her nose.

"I can't even, like, believe it, Cara. Who would do such a terrible thing? She was my, like, best friend, you know?"

"I don't know who could have done this, Laura. It's awful, for sure." Cara got up to pick up their coffees, and sat down again. "How did you know that I found her?"

"Ben Bauer told me? He said you were showing her listing on Carroll."

"Have you spoken to the police?"

"Yes. They came to my house last night. I hadn't seen her since, like, Monday?"

"When did you talk to her last?"

Laura started to cry again. "Thursday. On the phone. We had, like, a fight? That was the last time we talked, and I was like, yelling at her."

"Why, Laura? What were y'all fighting about?"

"Hannah could be so selfish! She always, like, did exactly what she wanted? Always got her way. And didn't care who it hurt? But I never thought she'd screw me over like that. I thought she was my friend." Tears ran down Laura's face. Cara reached for a napkin and handed it to Laura.

"What did she do?"

"She slept with Robby! It was only once, but she slept with my husband when I took the girls upstate last summer to the horse show." Laura started crying harder, and Cara sipped her coffee and waited. "I found their, like, text messages? I confronted her, and she tried to deny it, but she couldn't. She said it didn't, like, mean anything. Yeah, right. Not to her." Tears were rolling down her cheeks. "And now she's dead, and I think they think I did it! That policeman asked me where I was on Friday afternoon? Like I could kill my best friend? Jesus!"

"Well, did you tell them where you were?"

"Yeah, I told 'em. I was in Manhattan, Cara, taking the afternoon off for some retail therapy. I had Robby's credit card, and I was looking for something, like, expensive, you know?"

"Right. So who would be angry enough at Hannah to want her dead, Laura?"

"I don't know, but I'm probably not the only wife who got cheated on with her. And Ben knew it."

"He did? How do you know that?"

"He told me. But, I already knew. Last year when she was, like, sleeping with the counselor at Sadie's school." Sadie was Hannah's teenage daughter.

"Was she seeing anyone lately?" Even though Cara knew the answer, she wondered if Laura did.

"Yeah, but I don't know who. She wouldn't tell me, but I know she was. She'd started getting her hair straightened, and like, Botox treatments from my guy in Manhattan. I knew."

Cara started getting her coat on. "Well, I have to do an open house this afternoon. I better go. I'm sorry you lost your friend."

"They'll believe me, right? She was, like, my best friend. They'll realize I could never do that to Hannah, right?"

"That Detective Driscoll is a smart guy, Laura. I'm sure he'll figure it out. Just show him your credit card receipts."

Cara put her cup on the counter, and headed out the door.

She still needed to print floor plans for her open house. In Brooklyn's real estate market, hot and getting hotter, presentation was key. Cara's included professionally-shot photographs that she could include in marketing materials to hand out to potential buyers. She took pride in the show sheets and floor plans for her listings. It was important having buyers remember the properties. The four-story brownstone on 6th Avenue that was open for viewing on this afternoon was listed at $3.5 million, and like all her listings was getting a well-planned presentation. Back at her desk, she pulled up the file she wanted and hit print before heading for the color printer around the corner from where she sat. Standing at the printer waiting for copies to spit out of the Konica 480, Cara's colleague Tina Ross looked up from her task. "Cara, oh my gosh! I heard you found Hannah during a showing! How awful! What did your clients say? That must have been awkward." She laughed nervously. "Are they going to make an offer? Kind of puts the kibosh on your enthusiasm when you see a dead person in the kitchen, I imagine."

Cara stared at her and thought, *Tina, just stop now, please.* But Cara knew Tina too well to really expect that to happen. Tina continued. "But then, you've always got a story to tell about the first time you walked into the kitchen and found a dead body!"

Shaking her head, Cara reached for the floor plans in the slot, and said, "No, I don't think so. It's a crime scene, so I don't even know when we might be allowed in again. But my buyers didn't see her. I went in first alone, thank goodness."

Oh, God. I hope I don't have to go through that with every one at Corbin-Wheeler. If Tina knows I found her, it won't be long before everyone does. Wait—how did Tina know Hannah was found in the kitchen? Did Tina have a motive for murder? She shook her head, grabbed a folder and put the newly printed pages for the open house in it, and left the office. *I hope I don't go around thinking everyone in the office could be the murderer!* She was really glad to have some work to do. It would keep her from thinking too much about Hannah, and who might hate her enough to kill her.

Vanderbilt

By four o'clock that afternoon, open house over and follow-up emails accomplished, Cara was leaving the center part of the Slope and heading for home. She only had to go around her block a couple of times before she spotted someone pulling away from the curb right in front of her building—a parking spot!

Cara enjoyed Sunday evenings. She and Mary had a standing dinner plan, timing contingent on Cara's work schedule and any activities that Mary had with her grandchildren. Mary's daughter's family lived in the neighborhood adjacent to Park Slope to the south, Windsor Terrace, and Mary was very involved in their lives. Usually by at least 6:00 or so the two friends were deciding where to eat, and making a plan to get there. Their fallback choice was a casual Mediterranean place on Vanderbilt Avenue, Zaytoon's—that served the best hummus in the 'hood—just across Flatbush in Prospect Heights. An easy walk for both. They ate there so often that they called it "the Club". The waitstaff was efficient and friendly and so familiar with the women and what they always ordered, that they simply turned in the order when they saw them come in. Meeting up on the corner of Park Place and Vanderbilt, Mary gave Cara a hug and they walked the remaining blocks. Mary told Cara about the grandkids, and invited her to a school play that her older grandson was in. Cara knew Mary's family well. The two friends sat down at their favorite table by the window.

Mary spoke first. "Cara, how are you holding up? You must still be in shock."

"I'm okay, but I can't get the image of Hannah on that floor out of my mind."

"I don't doubt it. It's horrible. Do you think the police have any leads as to who the killer is? They must have been interested in the sex on the floor earlier in the day."

"I guess. I don't know where they are with suspects, but it seems to me there are probably a few. I mean, aside from agents who have been burned by her, who to me seem fairly unlikely—though I guess money is always a motive—there is her husband who could have been moved to murder. According to her friend, Laura Simonson in our office, Hannah was a serial cheater."

"Really? Did she say that?"

"Yeah, she did. She accosted me this morning at the

office and blurted that out. I guess Hannah's husband knows I found her, and told Laura. Laura, by the way, had had a fight with Hannah on Thursday when she found out that Hannah had been sleeping with her husband! Or had had a fling of some kind. Anyway, Laura said Hannah slept around, and that Ben Bauer knew it. I don't know, Mary. That's two people right there who could have wanted to kill her. I would assume the police are looking into them."

"Jeez, that's a perfect plot point."

"I guess so. Though I can't see Laura Simonson strangling Hannah. A knife in the heart maybe, or a gun, but choking someone to death with a scarf sounds, I don't know, difficult? She looks like she works out, but still . . ."

"Well, maybe Hannah's husband had just had it. One affair too many."

Cara looked thoughtful. "Yeah maybe. It's always the husband, isn't it?"

"Supposedly. But—regarding other agents. It doesn't necessarily have to be just about money. I mean reputation and ego could play a part here."

Mary had had a very successful career as a television writer, and plots were her forte. She and Cara were avid movie and theater-goers, and their discussions often centered around the writing. Mary was smart and pragmatic. Cara nodded. "You're right about that! Image is important in this business. Hannah had been at the top for a long time. Maybe someone was just sick of her, or had been number one before she came along. I wonder who that was? Shouldn't be that hard to scout out. It was before my time, but someone will have that backstory!" She went on to tell Mary about the chance sighting of Ben and the other man. "It was so strange."

Her friend nodded. "Strange indeed! Talk about cloak and dagger! Maybe he was another agent. Cara, if it's someone in your office, or at Corbin-Wheeler, I bet you can get to the bottom of it quicker than the police. You know these people. You are observant . . . and an astute listener."

Cara pondered that thought. "Maybe. Seems like a pretty long list of suspects to investigate."

The food arrived, and the two women surveyed their plates. Mary opened her napkin onto her lap, and said, "Well, be careful when you do. Someone killed Hannah for a reason. I don't want to lose my movie pal to a madman trying to tie up loose ends!"

Cara smiled. "Will do. I don't want you to lose your movie pal either. Bon appétit!"

7th Avenue

Mondays were for "light office work" as Tom often referred to it. It was a day to follow up with open house attendees or buyers that needed attention or second appointments. Cara planned to continue her search for the Fishers' perfect three-bedroom, as well as possibilities for a few other buyers she was currently working with. She tried to sleep in—a reward for the stressful weekend—but found herself awake at 6:00 a.m., trying to come up with a list of possible brokers who might have had it in for Hannah. Listings that she'd scooped, maybe, or deals that they might feel that they'd been shut out of. Who would know that? DeeAnne Martin, Hannah's assistant, had only been with her for slightly more than a year, but that was considered long-term for the position. Hannah went through assistants pretty quickly. She'd probably know the most recent conflicts, anyway. Definitely worth a conversation. DeeAnne and the other assistant, the new one (*what was her name?*) could probably shed some light on Hannah's professional enemies. But would they?—was the question. Cara headed into the office for a little light office work and some behind-the-scenes sleuthing. She stopped at the crepe shop for some muffins and a couple of lattes to-go. She would ply those assistants with lattes, or drink them herself.

She plopped her bag, beret and jacket at her desk and peeped around the corner to see the two young women at their desks, working at their computers.

"Hi, y'all. Hey, DeeAnne. Just wanted to check in with you and make sure y'all were okay. I brought y'all muffins and lattes, if you want them." Cara sat down at Hannah's chair, and offered up the bags.

DeeAnne, small and serious, turned to Cara. "Gosh, thanks, Cara."

"Sure. I wasn't sure if you'd be here this morning."

"Well, there are things to take care of. Hannah had quite a bit of stuff going on—several listings and such—and Patrick is helping us deal with it all."

"Like Carroll Street. It must be hard."

"Well, Patrick is actually speaking to the owners, and Beth is cleaning up the files, but lots of things have to be put into writing." The new assistant, Beth, barely looked up from the other desk.

"I still can't believe it. I keep wondering who could have

done this. I mean, we all have people we don't get along with, in this business, but to be so angry that you could kill is another story."

DeeAnne lowered her voice. "Well, it's no secret that a lot of people didn't like her. When I first started here, I'd mention I was her assistant, and more than one person would say, 'Poor you' or something like that. I almost quit a couple of times. But you get used to it, you know?"

"You seemed to get along with her, though. You've been here a long time."

DeeAnne shrugged. "When I first started, I really needed the job. And really she was a lot like my mother. Pick at you one minute, hug you the next. I knew how to ignore, or at least put up with, her moods. And she had her moments. She was generous, financially. I mean, she could afford to be, of course, but still . . ."

"Was there anyone lately that she had run up against? Maybe another agent?"

DeeAnne paused and took a sip of the latte Cara had brought. "Not really. Well, other than Laura Simonson. She and Laura had some kind of a big blow-up last week. I heard about it from several people, so it's not like it's a big secret or anything. I already told the police."

Cara nodded. "Yeah, I heard about that too. I meant, anyone that was really upset about a deal. Maybe the competitive aspect of this business just sent someone over the edge?"

The serious young woman shook her head. "Well . . .

last year she beat out Charlie Benton for Broker of the Year, and he said some pretty nasty things about her, but that seemed to blow over."

"Oh, right! Is that why he moved to the Fort Greene office?"

"Well, yeah. Although I'm not supposed to say that, but yeah. I guess it doesn't matter now. He said that Hannah's moral compass always pointed South. Whatever that means."

"Hmmm. Charlie Benton. Well, the pot and kettle analogy comes to mind there . . ."

DeeAnne looked puzzled.

"What will you do now, with Hannah gone?"

"We're both joining Sally Chang's team in Williamsburg."

"Oh, good for you!"

Cara wished them luck and went back to her own desk. There had been an email sent to all Corbin-Wheeler agents about Hannah's death, and another sent just to Brooklyn agents with the details of a memorial service at the Temple in Park Slope. It was scheduled for the following morning at 11:00. Patrick wrote to her, saying that the family would be receiving guests for shiva, starting Tuesday evening from 7:00 to 9:00.

Tom had sent an email to Cara, cc'ing Jim, asking if she wanted to have lunch after the services.

Yes, please, she'd replied. *And will you go to shiva with me at the Bauer's house tomorrow evening? We don't have to stay long.*

Jim's email answered, quickly. *Gosh, that sounds like fun, but no.*

Tom responded as well. *Sorry, Cara. No can do. We have theater tickets. But we'll meet you outside the Temple tomorrow around 10:45, for the memorial.*

Rats! She would be on her own, then, for the shiva. Or maybe she could meet up with Patrick. It felt like an obligation she should show up for, since she'd been the one to find Hannah's body, but she also wanted to have an opportunity to observe Ben Bauer up close. She was hoping that guilt or innocence would show on his face, but she wasn't sure if that was the way it went in real life.

Beth Elohim

The Temple of Beth Elohim stood in the heart of Park Slope on the corner of 8th Avenue and Garfield Place. It was grand and imposing, taking up both sides of Garfield Place, and played an important role in the community. Cara had attended events—readings and even a couple of AA meetings—in a few of the various rooms in the complex. Mary's granddaughter was in the child care program there. On the southern corner, people were now gathering in an icy rain outside what Cara thought of as the annex, but was really a huge auditorium. She recognized several brokers milling about, and looked around for Jim and Tom, but she was early, as usual, and knew she'd be waiting for them. Tom was notoriously late for almost everything. She often kidded him. "It's your only flaw. And I wouldn't notice, except I am always extremely punctual!" To which he would reply, "And that's yours!" Walking over had been a good idea, despite the weather. Her hat d'jour was a water repellant felt, but her Corbin-Wheeler umbrella had come in handy. Looking for parking was what those two were probably doing at that moment. Cara took out her phone and began checking emails. She felt sure any missives that came in this morning could wait, but she didn't want to talk to any of her colleagues about finding Hannah, and sticking her face in the phone was an attempt to be invisible. She knew, though, that word was getting around. Her conversation with Laura Simonson on Sunday had been overheard by more than a few agents, and that number would expand exponentially as the story got told.

Glancing around for signs of Tom or Jim, Cara caught sight of Lynette Carlisle exiting a Lincoln Town Car. Now there was someone she hadn't seen in quite a while. She'd actually not thought of her in a long time, either, though she now remembered that Lynette had retired and moved to Florida. Lynette was probably past seventy, still very fit and attractive, and had once been hugely successful at Corbin-Wheeler, though Cara knew she had worked for a few of the other agencies throughout her many years in the real estate business. She had been a broker at Corbin-Wheeler for a long time, and had mentored Hannah Bauer, now that Cara thought about it. *She* was most likely who Hannah had pushed out of the number one spot! But Cara was certain that, having brought Hannah into real estate, and more or less taught her the business, she'd been on board with Hannah's successful career. She had, no doubt, gotten referral checks for years from passing on her long-time clients to Hannah. Of course she would be here for this memorial.

Lynette was sharing an umbrella with a tall, very good-looking, much younger man whom Cara didn't recognize. New boyfriend? Maybe, maybe not. Cara knew Lynette only in the same way that most Corbin-Wheeler agents had known her in her last couple of years before she moved to Palm Beach—as a legend in the real estate business. She'd sold property in Brooklyn for more than forty years, long before computers and cell phones, and had made a great deal of money doing things the old-school way—with a desk, a telephone, and a well-curated Rolodex, kept under lock and key. She had still been in the office—though no longer seven days a week—when Cara had started with Corbin-Wheeler. Within Cara's first couple of years, she'd retired.

Lynette, on five-inch heels, and the man she was with, walked directly into the auditorium, without stopping to greet or acknowledge anyone at all. *That's where Hannah learned that arrogance*, Cara thought. *But Hannah had nothing on Lynette, that's for sure. That woman has a level of haute that's hard to achieve. It must take decades of practice.*

Tom and Jim strode up, at two minutes before the hour, looking dapper and well-put-together, as usual.

"Cara! You should have gone in. Why are you standing outside in this dreadful weather?" Tom hated rain. Winter, spring, summer or fall, he hated rain.

Jim shook his head. "He'll be late for his own funeral!"

"Maybe so, but I'm not late for Hannah's. Now let's go." The three walked into the auditorium, shook their umbrellas out, and took a seat near the back. It gave them a clear view of the mourners.

Cara lowered her voice. "Look, y'all. There's Lynette Carlisle."

"Wow. I haven't seen her in years. She looks just the same!"

Jim leaned in, voice quiet. "Nip and tuck! And still haughty after all these years!"

Tom frowned at Jim, but Cara stifled a giggle.

"I'm so glad they didn't do an open casket! I know it's supposed to be good for closure and all that, but it just seems weird to me. I don't see a casket at all." Jim whispered to Cara. She nodded, glad herself, though unsure of what protocol was for burial in Judaism. Cara had grown up in a basically fundamental congregation in a small West Texas town, but one to which she did not feel at all connected. She was not atheistic, just much looser in her spiritual beliefs than any religion she knew. Her AA practice and its adherence to spiritual openness was the only spiritual group in which she'd ever felt comfortable. But she hadn't—and still didn't—begrudge anyone their faith. Cara knew that life was often harsh, and comfort, rare. As she looked around at the fairly large group gathered in this room for Hannah Bauer's memorial, Cara found herself wondering if this would be a time and place for Hannah's friends and family to be comforted. She hoped so. Cara wondered, too, if the murderer was here. Since she felt that it had to be someone

Hannah knew, wouldn't that person be here today? She glanced around the large space and saw agents from quite a few Corbin-Wheeler offices, as well as some of the other real estate firms in the city. As she turned her gaze toward the door, she spotted Detective Driscoll in the last row, nearest the entrance. *Well*, Cara thought, *he must be wondering the same thing!*

After the service ended, two men wearing yarmulkes came forward and ushered the family out of their rows, closest to the front, followed by the emptying of each subsequent row. Cara watched as the congregants exited. Ben Bauer and his daughter Sadie, along with two women, who must be Hannah's sisters, and their husbands, and children. Others, obviously family, as well. Cara knew that Hannah had come from Saint Louis, originally, and that most of her family was still there. It seemed to be a large group. Then there was Laura Simonson, crying her eyes out, followed by none other than the overweight paper-eater she'd seen with Ben Bauer! That must be Laura's husband with their teenaged daughter in tow. Cara couldn't figure out how he was connected, except that apparently he had slept with Hannah. *Confusing!* They were followed by the CEO of Corbin-Wheeler, Alycia Cohen and her entourage.

As each successive row emptied and filed down the aisle, and out, Cara tried to imagine one of these people as a killer. There was Diane Wharton, the Fort Greene office's version of Hannah—the top broker from that office for a decade. And she was walking toward the exit with Charlie Benton, Hannah's nemesis who'd moved from Park Slope to Fort

Greene. *If Charlie Benton is the murderer, then Diane better watch her back*, Cara was thinking. *Laura, Charlie, maybe DeeAnne, maybe Tina—Jeez! The list of agents who wouldn't mind seeing Hannah dead really IS long!* If Ben Bauer didn't do it, though he was still her number one suspect, then which one of these mourners might be capable of murder?

Detective Driscoll was standing outside near the curb observing the people lingering. Cara approached him, as she opened her umbrella, and waited for Jim and Tom. They were talking to an agent from the Brooklyn Heights office.

"Detective Driscoll, how goes it?"

"Ms. Gerard, er, Cara—oh, it goes. I'm glad to run into you. I was going to call you. Can you stop by the station this afternoon or in the morning? I have some things on my mind. It would be good to talk to someone on the inside, so to speak."

"Sure. Tomorrow is better for me. I have an appointment this afternoon."

"That's great. Anytime before noon will work. Thanks."

Cara spotted Tom looking for her, and she waved to catch his eye.

"See you tomorrow." And she headed for 7th Avenue and lunch at Yamato with the guys.

8th Avenue

Cara looked in her closet, and considered what she should wear for a shiva. She could hear her mother's frowning voice saying, *Better to be overdressed, than underdressed, dear.*

Growing up in West Texas, she'd been exposed to what she supposed was the redneck equivalent of sitting shiva. When her father had died, her family's kitchen table had filled up with platters piled high with fried chicken and more Pyrex dishes of green bean casseroles than they could have eaten in a month. People crowded into the house, dressed like they were going to church, and talked quietly, and her grandfather had sat with her on the sofa, holding her hand for a long time. Since she'd moved to Brooklyn, Cara had been to two wakes: both in old-style funeral parlors that were standing room only and an open casket in the front. No food was involved, and both events were for AA friends, but she had noticed each time that the funeral parlors were right across the street from neighborhood bars, and Cara could imagine that that was no mere coincidence of location. Food or booze—something needed to be consumed during the grieving process. This afternoon, Cara had ordered a large loaf of banana bread from Ladybird Bakery. She would be taking that to the Bauer's that evening.

Eventually the decision was made for black jeans and a velvet tunic, with a soft mohair beret, her wavy hair loose, and that seemed just the right combination to Cara. Her understanding of what one did at a shiva was limited to what she'd gleaned from books and movies, so if there was to be any actual sitting, she wanted to be prepared. Mourners, apparently, usually sat on the floor or in low chairs, as a symbol of being "brought low" by their loss. She wasn't sure if this was just family or if all mourners were included, but in either case, she'd be ready. Shiva in Hebrew means seven, and traditional, more orthodox families might "sit shiva" for all seven nights, but she'd been told that the Bauers' would be hosting the memorial for this one evening only. Cara was primarily hoping to get a read on Hannah's husband. Ben Bauer might have had a motive for killing his wife, as Cara saw it, but since he'd been aware of her philandering for long term, what made this go 'round the one that might have made him snap? If Laura Simonson was right in her assessment of Hannah's behavior, it might be that Ben Bauer would have had grounds for divorce more than murder. *But who knows?* Cara pondered what kind of deception could make a husband angry enough to kill. Would it be more likely that just one time produced such a painful shock that it sent someone, blinded by rage, over the edge, or the repeated burn of betrayal over time that simply became too much to bear? She wasn't sure if either question had merit in this case, but she knew she was interested in the answer. *Or would he have hired Robert Simonson to kill her? Maybe that's the connection to Laura's husband. Oh, that doesn't make sense!*

She finished getting ready, and headed out the door, always the early-bird, well ahead of the time she wanted to arrive. And on this night, she was stopping first at a bakery, to pick up banana bread to take to the family.

Cara stood outside the Bauer's apartment building on Eighth Avenue, bakery box in hand, and waited for Patrick. He was coming from the Upper West Side of Manhattan, by subway, and had encouraged her not to wait outside, if he didn't make it on time. She, however, intended to disregard that suggestion. Cold or no cold, she didn't want to go in on her own. At least the icy rain had stopped.

"Hey, there!" Patrick Russo called out to Cara as he came around the corner from Berkeley Place. Patrick was young and smart and had been a welcome addition to the Park Slope office when he came on board a couple of years ago. He had an authentic way about him, and didn't play favorites, and Cara thought he was the best managing director Corbin-Wheeler had in Brooklyn. She really liked him, and his being here tonight was a perfect example of why. He showed up. And he showed up with enthusiasm. He knew

Cara wouldn't want to go alone, and she felt that he was coming in support of her, as much as for the respect he felt for his number one broker, and by extension, her family.

"Hey, Patrick. Thanks for meeting me."

"Of course! I'm glad we are doing this together. I have never been to a shiva before. You brought food? I wasn't sure what to bring."

"Oh, this is from both of us. I wasn't sure either, but I figured you cannot go wrong with banana bread." She lifted the box from the bakery that was just a few blocks away. "Actually, I called my friend Maxine Meyer, and she suggested this. Anyway . . . shall we?"

"Yep. After you." Patrick reached for the door, stepped back and gestured Cara into the lobby of the classic Brooklyn apartment building where Hannah Bauer had lived.

The doorman looked up from his desk. "Here for the Bauers?"

"Yes." Patrick nodded.

"6D."

"Thank you."

The two rode the elevator in silence to the sixth floor. The mirrors in the elevator were covered with cloth. Another shiva tradition. When the doors opened, Cara and Patrick stepped into the short hallway and walked to the door that had tall candles burning on either side. It was slightly ajar. To the right was a small table with a guest book, and a ceramic bowl that held torn black ribbons with straight pins stuck in them. Cara signed in and pinned one on her tunic, and then took another one and turned to Patrick.

"This is to symbolize the anguish of the death. Maxine says that instead of tearing one's clothes, you are supposed to wear this torn ribbon. A Jewish custom." She pinned it to his lapel. "Ready?"

He nodded, as they turned and entered the apartment. It was crowded but quiet. They paused just inside the foyer and looked around. At first Cara didn't recognize anyone, but as she scanned the crowd, she noticed a few agents that she knew and some of the people that she had seen—certainly family—at the memorial service at the temple. A tall, slender woman with long curly hair approached them and in a voice so low it was almost a whisper, said, "Hello, and thank you for coming. I'm Hannah's sister, Candice." She gestured them forward.

Cara shook her hand as she introduced herself and Patrick. "I am so sorry for your loss. I've worked with Hannah for about ten years, at the Park Slope office. We are all in shock, as I know you must be too."

The woman nodded, and led them to the dining room, where the table was covered with food of all kinds that people were eating. *I bet there are no green bean casseroles here*, Cara thought. A hutch to the side had a large coffee urn and cups and accoutrements, as well as bottles of wine and stemmed glasses. Cara walked through to the kitchen and handed the bakery box to the young woman, dressed in black pants and a white shirt with an apron—obviously service staff—then turned and rejoined Patrick.

Patrick whispered, "There's Syd." Patrick's boss, the regional vice-president of Corbin-Wheeler, stood looking out the window onto President Street. He turned as they approached, and gestured them over. Syd, tall and imposing, shook Patrick's hand and awkwardly hugged Cara. Quietly he said, "I can't believe it yet. It's just too much."

"Where are Sadie and Ben?" Cara looked around.

"They're in the living room, sitting on floor pillows. Sadie seems pretty stalwart, but Ben is a mess. I think Sadie is being strong for her Dad."

As they stood by the window, with the lit-up Park Slope view behind them, other guests arrived at the front door, and were met again, by Hannah's sister. Several people entered at once, but only one that Cara knew. It was Lynette Carlisle, dressed in black leather pants and a black fur coat, again accompanied by her tall, good-looking younger man. *She's a powerhouse, all right. What a presence!* Cara watched as Lynette surveyed the room, spotted Syd and headed their way. She wondered if Lynette would remember her. It had been at least seven years that she'd been gone. And Cara had been relatively new at that point.

Syd reached out his hand as the elegant older woman approached, and shook hers. "Lynette, how nice to see you, though I wish it could be under happier circumstances."

"Syd. I know. It's just terrible. Poor Sadie. Poor Ben."

Syd turned to Patrick and Cara. "I'm sure you remember Cara Gerard, an agent in the Park Slope office, but I'm not sure you've met Patrick Russo. He's the Managing Director now in Park Slope. Patrick, this is Lynette Carlisle. She was a star in your office for many years, and has been living in Palm Beach since she retired."

Patrick shook her hand and, ever-gracious, said, "Of course, I know you by reputation."

Lynette pulled her young man into the group and introduced him. "This is my son Hayden." Her son, tall and broad-shouldered, in his early forties and blonde, shook hands with Syd and Patrick, and nodded in Cara's direction. *Oh, her SON*. Cara blinked hard, taking notice as the man helped his mother off with her coat, and removed his own as well: His Brooks Brothers, camel hair coat. "I'll find a place for these, Mother. Be right back." Cara, heart pounding, couldn't take her eyes off him as he turned and walked away. Blond hair. Camel hair coat. Blond hair. Camel hair coat.

Cara brought her attention back to the conversation.

"Lynette, did you keep your home here?" Syd was asking.

"Oh yes. I could never give it up! I spend most of my time at the condo in Palm Beach, but I have to come to New York sometimes. I'm still on the board at Playwrights Horizons, and we had a meeting on Thursday. My brownstone is a double duplex. Hayden and his partner have the upstairs apartment. But I am back and forth fairly often."

Syd nodded. "Lynette has a beautiful townhouse on Montgomery Place and the Park. Just stunning."

"My perfect world. I can come to New York when the mood strikes, and I don't have to endure the cold if I don't want to. Good to see you all, and if you'll excuse me, I am going to speak with Ben and Sadie." Lynette took her leave and headed into the living room. Cara waited a moment and made her way in as well.

Cara kept her eyes on Hayden Carlisle for the next half hour. While she had come to observe Hannah's husband—who seemed throughout the evening to be sincerely in mourning—she couldn't get rid of the image in her head of the last time she had seen Hannah alive. And of the blond head that she had only a fleeting glimpse of, along with the camel colored coat that had been draped on the sofa in the apartment on Carroll. Detective Driscoll's prompt of closing her eyes and "seeing" the scene again, had brought that coat into memory, and Cara was now wondering if Hayden Carlisle just might have been the man on the rug with Hannah. She knew she had to find out more about him. As he headed to the end of the table with the wine uncorked and glasses at the ready, Cara intercepted him, and opened the conversation.

"Red or white?"

"Oh, red—thanks." He took the glass that Cara poured, and paused.

"Did you know Hannah well?" Cara asked.

"Oh, well, yes, I guess. She used to work with my mother, and you know real estate. It infiltrates everything you do. Twenty-four/seven. I think that's why I didn't go into it. Too much. No time off, really. But I got to know Hannah back when she first started with Corbin-Wheeler, and we stayed friends even after Mother moved to Palm Beach. And I've done some projects with her."

"Projects?"

"I'm an architect. I've worked with some of Hannah's clients. Brownstone renovations and such."

"Oh. Here in Park Slope?"

"Yes, and Cobble Hill. Brooklyn Heights. Here's my card, if you ever need an architect." He reached into the inside pocket of his jacket and brought forth a silver business card holder, swiftly handing her one.

"Carlisle and Croft. Thanks." Cara noted the quality of the business card. Velvety and tastefully extravagant with the Montgomery Place address. Even at a shiva the guy was a promoter. "I've worked in the Park Slope office with Hannah for the last ten years. I realized yesterday that I did my first deal at Corbin-Wheeler with Hannah. Seems like a long time ago. This whole thing has been so shocking. Just horrible."

Hayden nodded and took a sip of wine. His eyes scanned the room.

"Had you seen her lately?" Cara asked.

"We kept in touch."

"I know it's going to be hard for Ben and Sadie. Especially hard for a girl her age to lose her mom."

"Yes, I would think so." He was looking everywhere but at Cara and drinking his wine fairly quickly, she noticed. She got the distinct impression that Hayden Carlisle was starting to squirm. *Hard to talk about her personal life, Hayden? Did you forget she was a wife and mother?* Cara looked right at Hayden and said, "I was showing one of her listings on the day she was killed. The one she was killed in, in fact. I'm the one who found her."

Hayden looked up sharply. "You're kidding!"

Cara reached for the bottle and topped off his glass.

He was drinking fast. "I hope they find whoever did this quickly. The detective on this seems very smart. I think he'll figure it out. He's speaking with everyone who knew her or did business with her. I'm sure you'll be hearing from him."

"I don't know how much I can tell him, really. It's been a while since we worked on anything together. I've been mainly working in BedStuy. Lots going on over there." Cara nodded and lifted the bottle offering him a refill. He shook his head, finished the glass with one swallow, and set his glass on the table. "Cara, I think I'd better find my mother and head out. Take care."

Hayden walked away quickly. Cara watched him go. *That might not have been the smartest move—telling Hayden Carlisle that I found Hannah's body.* The more she thought about it, the surer she felt that this was the man she'd seen in flagrante delicto with Hannah. But didn't Lynette say he lived in her house with his partner? Did that mean he was gay? Or was she saying that he and his *business* partner officed there? The card he'd given her had the Montgomery Place address. *Very confusing. He sure seems to have inherited some of Lynette's snottiness, but that doesn't mean he's a killer. Does it?*

Cara looked around for Patrick. She needed to offer her condolences to Ben Bauer and Sadie. This was going to be tough, all 'round. Heading to the living room and seeing Hannah's daughter, brought up the loss of her own father when she was even younger that Sadie. It was a loss that she'd felt over and over her entire life. She noticed Ben with his arm around his child, and watched him wipe a tear way from his own cheek. Suddenly, Cara felt really sad. And a little guilty for considering him first as the perpetrator. Ben Bauer looked exhausted—and grief-stricken. She watched as people passed through to offer condolences. At one point the man broke down and cried. Unless he was a very good actor, she didn't see him killing his wife. Cara went over, offered her condolences, and turned to find Patrick. She was ready to go home. She caught his eye and started for the door. *Well, at least I have some ideas for Detective Driscoll tomorrow. And a few questions.*

The Precinct

The next morning around 10:30, Cara walked into the 78th Precinct with two large lattes from the French Cafe on Flatbush, and headed up the stairs to Detective Driscoll's office. Her mind had been working on possible killers all night, and she'd awakened with a whole list of people. This would be her second latte of the morning and she was looking forward to meeting with Driscoll and offering her insight. The detective opened his door just as she was about to knock. "Good morning, Cara. Thanks for coming by."

"No problem. I come bearing coffee." She handed him one of the to-go cups and dug in her jacket pocket for some sugars. "I hope I can help," she said as she dropped the packets on his desk. "And I was also hoping to spare you at least one cup of bad constabulary coffee." She removed her leather baseball cap and shook out her hair.

"Excellent! Thank you." Driscoll gestured for her to sit down, pried the top off the paper cup, took a long sip, made a satisfied face, and sat down behind his desk. He shuffled through the papers stacked in front of him. "I made some notes and was hoping you could give me your thoughts."

"It's certainly been on my mind. I am glad for the opportunity to talk."

"Can you tell me anything more about Laura Simonson? Have you heard anything more about the fight they had?"

"Well, I spoke to Laura over the weekend and she was really upset. She said she'd found out about an affair that her husband and Hannah had, which apparently prompted the phone call that I mentioned before. She said that they had been together only once, and that it was last summer, and that she had just found out. She said she'd found text messages and a second phone. I don't know anything more than that." Cara sat back and sipped her coffee. "Last summer, I had also heard that Hannah and Ben Bauer were separated and getting a divorce, but it never happened. I don't know if the two things were connected at all. Laura also told me that Hannah slept around. Again, I didn't know her well enough to know if that is true or not. But that's what Laura said. And she said that Ben Bauer knew it."

Detective Driscoll nodded. "Do you think that Robert Simonson could have been the man you saw with Hannah at the apartment on Carroll?"

"I don't think so. I don't know Laura's husband, but I

saw her with him and their daughter at the memorial service, and he has dark hair, and not much of it. I do have a strange thing that happened, and I can't figure it out."

The detective sat back with his latte and raised his eyebrows. Cara recounted seeing Laura's husband and Ben Bauer on Monday and Robbie's strange behavior after Ben biked away. "I recognized Hannah's husband from Facebook, but I had no idea that the other guy was Robert Simonson until I saw them at the memorial service. Anyway, my memory of that scene on the floor was definitely of a blond guy."

Driscoll leaned forward in his chair, with a thoughtful expression. "A blond guy . . ."

Hannah hesitated for a second, before she said, "I have an idea about that blond guy."

The detective cocked one eyebrow at her. "Oh yeah? Lay it on me."

"Well, I went to the shiva last night, and saw Lynette Carlisle. You may have noticed her at the memorial service. Short, spiky hair—a really attractive older woman? She came to the temple and to the shiva with a blond guy that turns out is her son. Lynette used to be a big-dog broker in the Park Slope office until she retired about eight or nine years ago. To Florida. She was a mentor to Hannah, I believe. Her son, as it happens, is an architect here in the Slope. Has known Hannah for quite a while apparently. He told me last night that he and Hannah had worked on a few renovation projects together. When I spoke to him, he seemed kind of nervous to me. Anyway, he has thick blond hair that seemed to ring a bell for me, and he was wearing a Brooks Brothers camel hair coat. It seemed all too familiar, but I can't be sure."

Detective Driscoll looked thoughtful. "Hmm. What's his name?"

"Hayden Carlisle. And he either lives in the upper duplex of Lynette's Brownstone on Montgomery Place or has his office there. I couldn't tell which from the conversation. But one or the other. And his mother mentioned his 'partner'. I didn't know whether that was his business partner or his life partner. Which was all kinds of confusing to me, if he's the guy who was having sex with Hannah, but whatever. I couldn't get blond hair, camel coat out of my head. Oh, and he gave me his card."

The police officer took it, jotted down the name and address and handed it back to Cara. He sat back, and gazed out the window in his office. It was small and high up, but brought some sky into the room.

"Anything else?"

"No, not really. There was one agent a couple of years ago who moved from the Park Slope office to Fort Greene, supposedly because of Hannah—but that's hearsay."

"And who was that?"

"Charlie Benton. Apparently he was in the running for Broker of the Year, but lost out to Hannah. Rumor has it there is very bad blood there. Beyond that, I don't know any more, really."

"I see. Okay, thanks Cara."

"I could ask around . . ."

"No. That's our job. But let me know if you get wind of anything that seems worth noting." His gaze returned to the window and he seemed to be rolling things around in his mind.

She stood and glanced up at the bit of sun that was coming in through the casement. "You could use more light, Detective."

"We could all use more light, Cara."

Cara smiled, and nodded, and left feeling that Detective Driscoll already knew most of what she had brought to the table, but maybe not. *Robbie? Hayden? Ben Bauer?* The more she thought about Charlie Benton, the more suspicious he seemed. Mary could be right. *Ego and money are big motivators in this world of New York City real estate.* She'd realized the source of the stress early on in her own career. *Big money and big dreams.* Cara had created a mantra of sorts for herself, when things started getting tense at work: *My stress level does not have to match the stress level of those around me.* And when she remembered to say it to herself, it helped. As a person in recovery, she couldn't afford to let this stress overwhelm her. The AA meetings helped, too.

She decided that she should try to talk to Charlie. It would be fairly easy to have a conversation with him. She also wanted to speak with Ben Bauer, one-on-one, though she had her doubts about his being a real suspect. It just didn't feel right to her. And she also knew she would see what else she could find out about Hayden Carlisle. Other people must know him, if he was working in Brooklyn. She wanted to know if he could be the guy rolling around with Hannah on her last day alive.

On an impulse, Cara stopped at the deli on the corner of Berkeley and 7th Avenue, and bought a tin of Earl Grey and, and then into Paper Source for a gift bag and a sympathy card. She walked over to the Bauer's apartment building, and stepped into the lobby. The doorman looked up as she asked to be announced to Ben Bauer. Nodding, he walked her to the elevator, and she rode to the sixth floor. Cara wasn't sure what she was going to say, but she'd wing it.

Ben was standing at his door as she exited the elevator. "Thanks for seeing me, Ben. I won't stay long, but I wanted to bring you some tea. Sometimes, it's the simplest things that bring comfort."

"Come in, Cara. That's very kind of you." He took the bag from her and looked inside. "Would you like a cup?"

"No, thanks. I just wanted to sit with you for a few minutes, if you felt like a bit of company. I knew Hannah in a whole different way from you and your family, and wanted you to know that I had a great deal of respect for her. I've been thinking about you. You know that I found Hannah, and I have been wondering about how I could possibly help."

Ben gestured to the sofa, and sat down himself. "It's been hard. Sadie is being the strong one here, but she and her mother were very close. I know she is suffering. And hearing what happened, and how it happened—well, it's a terrible thing." He started to cry quietly. "I'm sorry."

"Please don't be. It's an appropriate response."

"It was hard to hear she'd been, you know, with someone, that day. Did you see who it was? And I keep thinking—did he kill her? How terrible that would have been. I mean, to be hurt by someone you were . . ."

"I know, Ben. It could have been that, or someone else. I didn't see who she was with. You didn't know who she was seeing? Or is there anyone you suspect that would have wanted to hurt her? Had she been at odds with anyone lately that you know of? I feel if it were someone in our business, I could maybe observe or talk to in a way that the police might not be able to."

"No, I don't. And I don't know who it was that Hannah was seeing." He shook his head, as if to clear it. "It was not the first time. There have been a few, I guess. I don't know names, really. One of our friends, once, but we had such a row over it, I don't think she'd have done that again. Though Laura Simonson thinks Robby was sleeping with Hannah."

"He wasn't? He didn't?"

"No, absolutely not. She and Laura were friends, for Pete's sake. Laura is way off base with that. I tried to tell her, but she wouldn't listen."

"Well, Ben, there was a big blow out over the phone at the office that a few people overheard, and have assumed it was about Robby and Hannah. And frankly, Laura told me that. That she'd found a second phone of his, that proved it. No—?"

"Yes, Hannah had a second phone, too. The police found it. But it had nothing to do with sleeping with Robbie. I can promise you that."

Ben went to the refrigerator and pulled out a bottle of seltzer, pouring a glass for each of them. "She wasn't sleeping with him. It was somewhat habitual with Hannah, but you know, she was my wife. I loved her very much. And to the best of her ability, I know she loved me."

They talked quietly for a few more minutes, before Cara took her leave. She contemplated relationships, as she walked back to her apartment. *Love is complicated*, she thought. *And sometimes a burden.*

5th Avenue

New York City was always changing, and that was what Cara found most interesting about it. It seemed that every few years or so, a neighborhood in any borough, but of course she was most aware of Brooklyn, became a completely different place. New nationalities arrived, or demographics shifted, or meteorological crises occurred to cause a neighborhood to evolve entirely, it seemed, from what the inhabitants had grown used to, to a place they no longer felt was completely "theirs." Interlopers eventually became old-timers. Beginning with the Dutch who settled Manhattan, and then on and on, every three or four generations, speeding up as the world sped up, the change was continual. And just as uncomfortable to the former immigrants as their immigration had been to the citizens who came before. Restaurants, once landmarks, made way for cuisine more acceptable, or interesting, or desirable in some way to the new settlers. Change was inevitable. The great thing, in Cara's view, was that all who came before left their mark, in some way. Italian bakeries were still there, in Cobble Hill, offering up cannolis and baba ricotta. Farrell's remained on the corner of 16th Street in Windsor Terrace (since 1932—according to a sign in the window) serving the old Irish dockworkers a pint at 8:30 in the morning, though it had been joined right across the street by a brew pub that served "pub fare" as well as twenty-nine varieties of artisanal beers. Park Slope's Greek diners still thrived amid the growing number of burger bistros and coffee bars. And of course, the architecture in Brooklyn was varied as well. The gothic churches in the neighborhood, built in the late 1800s, as well as the brownstones for which Park Slope is most known, brought an air of old world sensibility to the neighborhood that was becoming home to a new generation of New Yorkers thoroughly entrenched in the modern. Cara loved it all. The old, the new, the overlap.

Walking along Fifth Avenue, the street that Mary O'Brien had told her was too dangerous to stroll after 5:00 when she and her new husband first moved to Brooklyn in the early seventies, Cara was on her way to meet Tom and Jim at Stone Park Cafe for dinner. The three friends liked to try new places around the neighborhood, so just about once a month, they picked a newly opened restaurant, or one they didn't usually frequent. This small and quietly elegant eatery sat on the corner across from Gabriel Byrne Park, and provided a wide window to watch the comings and goings of Park Slope's inhabitants, as well as a solid reputation for food well-prepared.

"I'm having the pear salad, for sure. And either the Swiss chard raviolini or the cod. I can't decide." Cara closed her menu, and looked up at her friends.

"What are y'all thinking?"

"Stuffed Branzino."

"Tenderloin."

Cara smiled. "Oh good. I want a bite of all that."

"Me too. Done." Tom shut his menu and gestured for the waiter.

Food ordered—Cara went with the raviolini—Jim and Tom looked across at Cara, and waited. Jim spoke first. "Okay. Spill the beans."

"Not if you don't want to, Cara, but we are dying to talk about this." Tom piped in. "Who do you think killed Hannah? I have some ideas, but you go first."

"Well," Cara began, "I don't think it's a real short list of suspects, do you? I mean, not to speak ill of the dead, as they say, but the girl was not well-liked. Of course, 'not well-liked' shouldn't get you murdered."

"Or else there'd be a whole lot more murders in real estate offices!" Jim offered this up while he munched on a thick slice of bread from the basket that the waiter had just delivered.

"But resentment runs deep sometimes." Tom pointed out. "You know who could have a motive? Her assistant, DeeAnne. Hannah treated her like crap."

Jim chimed in, "Maybe, but she's such a little person. I can't see her overpowering Hannah. She would have to shoot her. Or stab her, maybe. Could you tell how she was killed?"

Cara shrugged. "Maybe the opportunity just presented itself and the resentment took over. I don't think it was premeditated. I think she was strangled with her own red wool scarf, although I'm not supposed to say that, so keep it under your hat. Nobody came in with a gun or a knife." Cara recalled the scarf around Hannah's neck. "Or maybe the sex was kinky, you know, and just went too far—what's that called? Erotic asphyxiation."

"I don't think so," Tom said. "I think people who are into that use specific items. Silk cords. Like that."

"Honey, how do you know?" Jim looked quizzically at Tom.

"Oh, I don't really. But I've been to a sex shop or two. They have displays and such. Anyway, I just don't think they'd use a red wool scarf. It's not sexy."

"Well, that fight Laura had with Hannah on the phone was about the fact that Hannah had slept with her husband. That might make Laura want to kill her."

Tom raised his eyebrows, saying, "Wow, really? They've been friends for a long time."

Jim sipped his sparkling water, and smirked. "What are friends for?"

"Laura also told me that he wasn't the first and that Ben Bauer knew it. Suspect number one, I reckon. Maybe he followed her to Carroll Street and caught them in the act."

She told her friends about seeing the two husbands together on the bench. It sounded more absurd, every time she told it.

Jim frowned. "Ben would be the obvious choice, for sure. But what would he and Laura's husband have to say to each other if that was between them? And why would he eat paper? What is that eating disorder called? There's a name for that. A syndrome, or something."

Cara reached for a breadstick. "No idea. But Ben Bauer looked like he was really grieving to me at the shiva last night. It felt so sad. And I went by again this afternoon, and took him a box of tea. I don't think he's our guy, y'all. He seems so hurt."

The three friends chewed thoughtfully.

Cara swallowed. "And you know Charlie Benton transferred to the Fort Greene office because of Hannah, is what DeeAnne told me. That guy could have been holding on to a grudge."

"I remember that. But who was the guy she was with when you saw them getting it on that day? Any ideas?"

"Actually yes. That guy that Lynette Carlisle came to the memorial service with—turns out that's her son, Hayden. I thought maybe it was a new younger boyfriend, but no. Thick blond hair and he showed up to the shiva, wearing a camel-hair Brooks Brothers' coat. Remember I saw a camel colored coat on the sofa the first time I went in? I think it might have been him."

"Did you get a chance to talk to him?"

"Yeah. But only enough to find out he'd known Hannah

a pretty long time, and to get the impression that he was a little nervous. He didn't want to talk to me about Hannah. At least that's what I picked up."

"What do we know about him?" The food arrived and the three friends paused in their conversation long enough to take first bites. "Hmmmm." "Oh wow." "I want a bite of that raviolini. That looks great."

"Apparently, Hayden Carlisle is an architect. Oh, wait—I have his card." Tom stabbed a piece of ravioli as Cara reached into the side pocket of her bag and pulled out the elegant business card, handing it to Jim. "Carlisle and Croft. Their office is in the upper duplex of Lynette's brownstone on Montgomery Place, but I don't know whether they live there, too, or if he's gay, or what. Have you ever heard of them?"

"Maybe." Jim reached for his cell phone and googled the name on the card. "Oh, yeah. I don't know if I know Hayden Carlisle, but Will Croft is that guy, Tom, that was on the board at Human Rights Campaign, when we were volunteering at the Brooklyn fundraiser year before last, remember? Really tall, kinda handsome in a George Clooney kind of way. Remember?"

"No, not really."

"Yes, you do. He wore a tuxedo with a top hat to the gala."

"Oh yeah. I remember him. That's Hayden Carlisle's business partner? Aren't they a couple? I'm pretty sure they are." Tom took another bite.

Cara shrugged. "I don't know. But if they are, maybe it

wasn't him I saw rolling around in the heat of passion with Hannah."

"Well, it still could have been. Some people are, shall we say, versatile?"

"Hmm. I don't know. It's just that when I saw him at the shiva the other night, I saw his thick blonde hair, and he was wearing a camel hair coat, and it struck a chord, you know? Seemed to trigger something for me."

"Well, did he seem like someone who could kill another human being?"

"Listen, I don't know! But if we are saying it wasn't premeditated, I think anyone might get worked up enough to murder under the right—or wrong—circumstances. That's why they're called 'crimes of passion', right?"

"I guess." Tom poured everyone more sparkling water. "I really can't picture being angry enough to kill, myself."

Jim looked up. "To kill yourself?"

"To kill comma, myself. Though actually, I am more of a suicide person than a homicide person, I think."

Jim and Cara looked at each other and frowned. "I don't want to hear that," Jim exclaimed. "Honey, that makes no sense to me at all. You'd get so upset at somebody else that you'd kill yourself? Not me. I'm telling you right now, they'd be the one to go."

Cara looked at them both, and chuckled. "Well, good to know. I'm glad y'all have both been in therapy long enough to know yourselves so well!"

On the Cusp

The next morning Cara made her own version of a cafe latte. Cara and coffee had a long and satisfying relationship, and Cara had, over the years, enjoyed it many different ways from dark and bitter (just like her first husband, she often joked) to her current mandatory brew—at least when she prepared it at home—of a very strong and rich French-pressed with a hand-frothed topping of hot milk. She moved to the living room and sat in the rocker by the window. Her first floor apartment was not large and didn't offer a glamorous view of anything, but the beautiful inlay wood floors and the prewar style of it, along with her comforting look into the building's courtyard and the perfect location in a neighborhood bustling with good restaurants and proximity to Brooklyn's renowned Botanic Gardens, Art Museum, and of course Prospect Park, was just the right space, as far as she was concerned. Cara loved waking up in her comfortable apartment on the cusp of Prospect Heights and Park Slope. She felt very lucky, indeed.

Cradling the warm cup and appreciating the quiet—no neighbor kids' voices yet, in the hallway getting off to school—Cara thought about what she really knew about Hannah Bauer: Her status as Park Slope's top realtor, her role as a mother to a teenager, and her unfaithful marriage to an investment banker were the "facts". Those facts needed backstory details fleshed out if Hannah's murder was to be solved.

Cara couldn't help but think that the death of this woman had something to do with something besides her jealous husband. Ben Bauer had seemed genuinely sad at both the memorial service and the shiva. Not frightened or closed off in any way. Sad and bereaved. She felt sorry for him, and for their daughter. Ben and Hannah would never get to make up—never have the opportunity to get back to the love that they surely had had for one another once. They would never fix their marriage. And they would never get to make things right for a child who had nothing to do with such selfishness. Sadie would never cry on her mother's shoulder. Hannah would never dance at her daughter's wedding.

Laura Simonson had a motive. She believed that her best friend had slept with her husband. That could turn a friend into an enemy. And Hannah's assistant, DeeAnne, had been overworked and humiliated on numerous—and witnessed—occasions. She could have wished her dead, but was such a small woman that Cara was having a hard time picturing her overpowering Hannah Bauer long enough to wrap a scarf around her throat and strangle her. *Unless she had help. Maybe the other assistant helped. Beth, isn't it? Then it would have to have been premeditated, wouldn't it? And they wouldn't go to a murder, would they, without a weapon? And what about her real estate nemesis, Charlie Benton? And Hayden Carlisle—Mr. Blond Hair? Maybe he wanted more than an affair. Maybe she wanted more than an affair. Gosh, that's a lot of maybes!*

Cara took the last sip of the milky coffee from her cup, and reached for her phone to pull up the app for her guided meditation. She sat for a few restful minutes listening to calm.com. As she walked to the kitchen for another round of coffee, she realized that Mary was right. She knew what she had to do. What she'd actually been doing since the memorial. She was going to do the things that made her a good realtor. She was going to pay attention to everything people did and said, regarding the murder—and follow up with Hannah's assistants. She was going to talk to Laura Simonson again for more information. And she was going to find out more about Lynette Carlisle's son and Charlie Benton. She needed to find out where they'd been when Hannah was murdered. Cara *was* a very good listener and she was going to do just that. And she had imagination. Cara was sure that she could creatively analyze the circumstances and come up with a solution. Or at least, offer up some insight to Detective Driscoll. These particular skills she had brought with her when she became a realtor, and they had been honed, and had served her well in bringing buyers and sellers to a meeting of the minds when she negotiated purchases. She had also learned to listen by sitting in AA meetings for over two decades. It was a valuable skill for a great many reasons. Pouring more coffee into her cup, Cara felt committed. She was going to do her best to get to the bottom of this, find out who killed Hannah Bauer, and get this deal closed!

Al Di La

The day was bright and breezy as Cara stepped out of her building and onto the street. She wore a red cashmere beanie that matched her dark red Frye booties. It was cold and weather.com predicted snow tonight. *Wouldn't that be lovely?* She had plenty to do today at the office. This whole thing with Hannah's death had cost her time that she normally would have been working on following up on her listings and finding new possibilities for her buyers. The Fishers as well as a few others needed some attention if she was to find them their dream home. And that was a job she took seriously.

Cara was also determined to find a way to get to the Fort Greene office and speak to Charlie Benton. Or at the least, to give him a call. She would take a look at his web page and see if he had anything new that would appeal to any of her buyers. That would be a place to start, in approaching him. Charlie was definitely not her favorite human, though she didn't know him well. They had done a deal together a couple of years ago, on a Fort Greene condo, and it had gone well enough. She knew that he could be a bit of a pill, or maybe a downright asshole, depending on your state of mind. Cara had ended their deal on good terms however, so she felt all right about reaching out to him. *Anyway*, she thought to herself, *good thing I did my meditation this morning!*

She walked briskly up 7th Avenue toward the office. The phone in her pocket began ringing, and glancing at the unfamiliar number on its face as she grabbed it, she answered as she always did, "Cara Gerard."

"Oh, hi, Cara," said a vaguely familiar voice. "This is Lynette Carlisle. How are you?"

Surprised, Cara blinked and answered, "Well, I'm fine, Lynette, and you?"

"Very well, thank you. I know you must be busy, and this is short notice, but could we meet for lunch today? I have something I would like to discuss with you."

"Um, sure. Could we make it around 1:30 or 2:00? I am just on my way to the office."

"That's fine. How about Al Di La at 2:00?" Lynette had chosen a very nice Park Slope restaurant with a pricey menu and limited seating, but Cara could imagine that Lynette was a regular there when in town, and a table would be made available for her.

"Sounds lovely. I will see you there. Two o'clock." She hung up, puzzled as to the reason for this invitation. *Well, this should be interesting. What is on her mind, and what does she want with me?*

Cara spent the morning combing thru the multiple listing website that provided all the realtors who were members access to the listings in all the boroughs in New York City. She was looking on behalf of several buyers, including the Fishers. All her clients were important to her, and she thought that right now was not the time to let any new listings fall thru the cracks—especially for Dan and Molly Fisher. Being even peripherally involved in a murder investigation was enough to put anyone off their game, and she didn't want them to lose their enthusiasm for the search. More and more would be coming available, as the Spring market heated up, and Cara was determined to find just the thing for this couple. She figured they'd lost the taste for 862 Carroll Street, having seen someone having sex on the floor, and then knowing that later that same someone had died in roughly the same spot. But maybe not. People could stretch a great deal for the right piece of real estate in this city. From her experience, she was aware that many relationships were made or held together by a good apartment at the right price. Cara decided she'd ask about how soon she could show that apartment. *You never know*, she thought. *You just never know.* And sure enough, she saw that Charlie Benton did have a couple of things that might be of interest to them. These were in Prospect Heights—the recently more tony neighborhood to the north of Park Slope. She'd give him a call after lunch, and see if she could speak to him directly.

Cara opened the door and stepped into Al Di La right at 2:00. Coming in from such a bright day, she didn't see Lynette right away. But she was there. And she saw Cara. She was in the far corner, facing the room. As Cara removed her Ray-Bans and her eyes adjusted, she saw the woman raise a hand to gesture her over. Cara was very much aware of Lynette's scrutiny as she walked toward the table, and was determined to pay as close attention to Lynette as this older woman seemed to be giving to her. The reason for this lunch was puzzling to her, and Cara felt certain it would be interesting, but sitting down with someone she didn't know well at all was a bit disconcerting. She decided, as she slid into her chair, that she would do much more listening than talking. But she would open the conversation. A simple question put forth frankly, would hopefully cut thru any idle chitchat that would delay the breaking open of this mystery of why she'd been invited to share a meal with the former powerhouse of the Park Slope office.

"How nice to see you again, Lynette. How can I help you?"

Lynette Carlisle raised an eyebrow, and gave a little laugh. "Well, I'd heard you were very straightforward. That's excellent! Let's order, and I'll tell you what's on my mind." She reached for the menu and gestured to the waiter at the same time. Both women ordered quickly: salads and a bottle of San Pellegrino. Lynette ordered a glass of chardonnay, and waited for Cara to order from the wine menu. Cara waved the waiter off, sat back in her chair, and smiled her best Mona Lisa smile.

Lynette leaned forward, elbows on the table. "I heard you were the one who found Hannah. That must have been awful!"

Cara nodded. "Yes, it was."

"Do you have any idea who could have done this?"

Cara shook her head. "None at all."

"Well, I'm sure the police will find out who it was."

Lynette paused for a split second, and took a breath. "You know, I moved to Park Slope in 1975. There were only two brokers here then, and there was no such thing as a multiple listing service in Brooklyn. Manhattan, yes, but not Brooklyn. People still saw it as an "outer borough" and Park Slope wasn't even close to what we know today." She paused, took a sip of her chardonnay, and leaned back in her chair. She was clearly just getting started.

"I joined Patricia Gallo, who had a one-person office on 7th Avenue where Park Properties is now, and we just took over Park Slope. The only other broker in the neighborhood was Harvey Hammond, and he didn't do a tenth of the business we did. Patricia taught me everything she knew, and we put her name on just about every listing in the neighborhood. Attorneys begged us to work with them. Other small offices opened up, because of the amount of real estate that we sold, but really, they couldn't keep up. And they mostly came and went. We were selling brownstones and co-ops for what at the time were huge amounts of money. Buckets! We made the market in Park Slope. We made Park Slope what it is today. And then the big companies noticed. And they wanted a piece of the pie. Patricia was over seventy and wanted out of the business, so when Corbin-Wheeler offered to buy her out, she went for it. And of course, they wanted me to run the office for them. So I did for a few years, and they took over Brooklyn. Opened offices in Brooklyn Heights and Fort Greene. Became the biggest company in the city. And then, of course, they wanted someone younger to run Park Slope. Which was fine. It wasn't really fun anymore, anyway. So I went back to sales. Which is what I'm best at, of course. But I got tired of it." She paused. "Sick of it really."

Lynette sat back in her chair and reached again for her wine glass. "When Hannah Bauer first got into the business, I was thinking about my next chapter, and I made a deal with her. I taught her how to sell real estate, and fed her my listings—I mean I didn't give her my Rolodex, but I showed her the ropes, and gave her a very generous referral fee, and as you know, she prospered. You think she was the number one broker in Park Slope all by herself? No way. I made her number one just like I made Park Slope." Lynette sipped her chardonnay. "Don't get me wrong. She had drive. And she was smart. But my sellers and my buyers moved her way up the ladder fast. I have been feeding her business ever since. I come to New York when I have to, but I like the Palm Beach lifestyle. It has worked out well for both of us. I've been in Florida full time for almost ten years. And Hannah has been the Number One Broker for just that long. Had been the Number One Broker."

The waiter arrived with their plates, and Lynette ordered another chardonnay. Cara unfolded her napkin and lifted her fork. "Bon appétit!"

Lynette smiled. *"Buon appetito!"* They both ate in silence for a moment. "So what does this have to do with you? See? I'm straightforward, too! I have a proposition for you, Cara. Now that Hannah's gone, I am wondering if you would want to be my go-to person here in Brooklyn. I still have a great many people who know me, and come to me to get their deals done. Sydney speaks very highly of you. He says you are smart and that you know what you are doing and have done very well for yourself. My people are mostly high-end clients, and often these people need quite a bit of hand-holding. And they are used to having their way. But they also need someone who can stand up to them—and for them. I can connect you with both buyers and sellers, Cara. And I will basically be behind the scenes with whatever help you need, of course. But I won't get in your way. I think I can help you make a lot more money in this business. I am in a position to make sure we both make money. We can work out the split—or I can start you with what Hannah started with—but what do you say? Will you think about it?"

Cara swallowed a bit of kale she'd been chewing and took a drink of water. All kinds of whistles were going off in her head. *This is how Hannah Bauer did so well? She had all those listings over the years because of Lynette?* The older woman was essentially offering to partner up—albeit long distance—with Cara. *Why not someone more "New York"? Where was this coming from?*

As if she heard Cara's thoughts, Lynette spoke again. "You know, Cara, I think that 'Southern hospitality' thing you've got going might be just the ticket to blend with my 'tough love'."

Cara felt instinctively that there was something else besides real estate underlying this proposition from Lynette. But whatever was going on here, Cara decided she couldn't pass up an opportunity to find out more about Lynette Carlisle, and perhaps her connection to Hannah. Maybe this could lead to further conversation regarding Hayden Carlisle. And certainly, more business was always good! Quickly, Cara made her decision. "Gosh, Lynette, of course, I am flattered! And it sounds like an opportunity I cannot afford to at least discuss further. I have to get to an appointment now, but can we make a plan to meet again after I have had a bit of time to formulate some questions about the specifics of it all? I would love to talk again."

Lynette signaled for the check, and smiled. "Absolutely! Why don't you give me a call tonight and we can set up another meeting. I am planning to be here for a week or so." The waiter brought the check which Lynette insisted on paying, and the two women exited together, and parted ways at the corner. Cara headed back to the office, and thought again. *What was that about? What does Lynette really have on her mind?* And as had been said to her many times over in her years of recovery in AA, she knew the only answer that mattered: More will be revealed.

The office was almost empty when Cara returned, but Tom was at his desk, working, and looked up as she sat down at hers. "I always love that color red on you." He paused. "What's cooking, Cara? You okay?"

"Thanks. Yes. Interesting day. How about you?" She dropped her purse and jacket at her desk, and headed for the office kitchen. "I need a latte. Want one? I'll make 'em."

"Sure! Use half and half for me, though, will you?"

"Of course. I know you!" In the kitchen, outfitted with a top-of-the-line Nespresso machine and an electric frother, she found the dairy products in the frig, and did her best barista. She sipped the hot milky mixture and headed back with the two cups in hand.

Tom looked up over his reading glasses. "Where've you been? I'm hungry. Want to go grab a bite at Yamato? I guess we've missed lunch, but at least we have also missed the kids." Yamato, a block away, was their default for lunch. The sushi was good and reasonable, and the service exemplary. The only downside was that the elementary school kids from P.S. 321 all rushed in at 12:00 every day, to order sushi to go, and the noise level went up several decibels. It sounded like a high-pitched squeal that could cut through any conversation. Park Slope children knew their tempura rolls from their futomaki, but they were still kids-without-parents at the local eateries around the neighborhood at lunchtime. Tom and Cara and Jim did their best to avoid eating at that particular time, especially at a place as intimate as Yamato.

"No, thanks. I ate lunch already. With Lynette Carlisle." Cara waited a beat before looking over at her friend. Tom stopped typing, mid-sentence, removed his specs, and turned to face Cara, eyebrows raised.

"Wha-aat?"

"Yes. At Al Di La." She smirked. "She just called me up out of the blue this morning, and asked me to meet her for lunch."

Tom's raised eyebrows moved into a furrowed frown, as he pondered the possible implications of a lunch invitation from Lynette. "I didn't know you even knew her. You started right about the time she was phasing out, right?"

"Yeah, that's right. I actually met her, officially, the other night at the Shiva at the Bauer's. I, of course, knew who she was, but I got the impression she didn't know me from Adam. I don't know what to say, but it was definitely an interesting lunch." She lowered her voice and scooted into the chair beside Tom, where Jim usually sat. "Get this." Speaking in a low and quiet voice, she laid out Lynette's proposal.

"Wow." Tom shook his head. "I guess I should have gone to that Shiva! You're gonna make millions! You said yes, right?"

"Well, I told her I would think about it, and formulate some questions. And I was thinking I should talk to Patrick about it. Get his take on it. See what kind of deal Hannah had with Lynette, money-wise. But yeah, seems like something I shouldn't pass up, right?"

"Jeez, Cara, I would have had a hard time not saying yes right away! But how can you miss? I mean a steady flow of high-end referrals could definitely be a game changer. So can I borrow twenty dollars 'til payday?" That was a standing joke that Cara and Tom and Jim had. Real estate sales could be quite lucrative, of course, but one could go months without a paycheck, as well. An agent learned fairly early on how to manage money—that, or one could expect to flounder. For one thing, it is a seasonal business. For another, even when the work is steady, from start to finish, a real estate transaction usually takes a minimum of ninety days to close, because of co-op boards and mortgage processing. All-cash deals are only about 20 percent of the business. The guys and Cara would tease each other when one of them was busy and the others weren't. "Can I borrow twenty dollars 'til payday," really meant "good for you, you're on a roll."

"I know. It sounds good." She took another swallow of coffee.

"But—?"

"I can't help thinking that there's something else going on here. I mean, why me? My grandfather said if something seems too good to be true, it probably is, right? Why not Laura Simonson or . . ." Cara shrugged.

Tom interjected. "Well, come on, Cara! I mean, really—who's going to pick Laura over you? You are smart, and a really good agent. And you know—she just saw you and met you again, so you were on her radar. I think it was a good choice on her part. I'm happy for you! What's that old saying about not looking a gift horse in the mouth? Did your grandfather ever say that one? I'm not sure what that means, but if you ever need any help with your buckets of listings . . ." He smiled and turned back to his work.

Cara moved back to her own desk and stared at her computer, trying to get on board with Tom's evaluation of Lynette's motives. She knew she would take this offer. And she wanted to take this offer at face value. But she couldn't help thinking that there was something here she couldn't see. Something underlying. She could smell it.

Park Place

It had been a very productive day and an interesting one as well. Cara arrived back home that evening after hitting an AA meeting where she could spend an hour listening to people who had been beaten by alcohol, and had found a way to use that experience to seek connection to a better way of life. The best thing AA had done for her, other than a clear path to not drinking, she felt, was to give her a more open mind: to try things that she didn't believe would work to deal with anger and loss—and joy, for that matter. Life was a series of experiences, and for the first part of her adulthood, she had felt so ill-equipped to maneuver through them. So alcohol had been her answer. Since getting sober, she'd found a way to feel more comfortable in the world and handle baffling situations. At least most of the time.

Baffled was still how Cara was feeling about Lynette Carlisle's proposal to channel real estate referrals to her. Her conversation late in the afternoon with Patrick Russo had been encouraging. Apparently, in the last couple of years, the four or five deals that had come to Hannah from Lynette had all been in the three to five million dollar range. Definitely worth doing, even with a commission split that favored Lynette, which is how Cara assumed Lynette would want it. Patrick had advised her to negotiate a 50/50 deal to begin, which was the deal that Hannah had. Patrick had told her that Hannah's first few years working with Lynette had been with less, but there had been many more deals then. The longer Lynette was more or less out of the business, the fewer deals she'd sent Hannah. That was fine by Cara. Her own business was good and growing, but any additional buyers or sellers that came her way would be, of course, valued. And if she found she didn't like doing business with Lynette in this way, she could always bow out. She did continue to wonder why Lynette had brought this offer to her. She would like to think it was because she was smart and good at her job, but she couldn't help a bit of wariness. Still. . . .

Scrolling thru her phone for Lynette's number, her thoughts returned to Hannah. Less than a week after her death, and her business was being divvied up, presumably her bills were getting paid, her family was dealing with life without her. For better or for worse, this is what happened when someone died. Life moved around, shifted, and went on. And that's probably how Cara would have treated Hannah's death, too, except for the fact that Hannah didn't just die. She was murdered. And Cara had found her.

She texted Lynette to set up another meeting for Saturday to discuss their business arrangement. Cara had requested the conference room for 11:00. Aside from the referral conversation, she also planned to talk to Lynette some more about Hannah. Maybe this woman who knew Hannah well could provide some backstory that would help solve this. *If I'm going to benefit, in this way, from Hannah's death, I'm going to at least try to find out who did this to her. I'll talk to Laura again, too. Somebody here knows something!*

7th Avenue

It had been one week exactly, since Cara had opened the door at 862 Carroll to find Hannah dead on the kitchen floor. She wondered how Detective Driscoll was faring in the investigation. Hopefully he was well on his way to finding who did this. She decided that it couldn't hurt to touch base with him. Sitting at her desk at the office the next morning, she reached into her bag for his card. *Detective Dean Driscoll*, it read. *Sounds like a TV cop show character.*

Detective Driscoll picked up his phone right away. "Driscoll." She smiled. *He is certainly all business. Well, that's good. What a hard job.* Cara had a saying that she tried to remember when things got stressful in her work—and they often did: *It's real estate. It's not life and death.* But for this guy, it was. And really only death. He was a homicide detective, after all.

"Hi, Detective Driscoll. It's Cara Gerard. I'm wondering if you've had any movement on who killed Hannah Bauer. I, of course, can't get it out of my mind."

"Oh, hello, Cara. We are working on a couple of leads, but nothing concrete."

"I just wanted to check in. If there's anything I can do to help, since I do speak real estate, I am available. If you need me."

"Will do, Cara. Thanks. And if you find out anything new, circle back." He hung up, and Cara felt slightly disappointed that Detective Driscoll hadn't offered up any more information. She wondered what leads he was pursuing. Maybe that was just his way of brushing her off. *Hmmm.*

Checking her emails, Cara saw that the conference room for 11:00 on Saturday had been confirmed by the office receptionist. She texted a confirmation to Lynette. *Oh good.* That would give her plenty of time to get a referral form from admin and write down her basic understanding of their arrangement that they could both sign. That had been Patrick's suggestion. *Get it in writing.*

Next, she wanted to talk to Laura Simonson again, as well as Hannah's assistants. Both of them. Hopefully they were still working out of the Park Slope office, but she would drive to Williamsburg, if necessary. Cara knew and liked several of the agents in that office, and she always enjoyed seeing the managing director, who had started out in the business with Cara.

Scrolling thru her emails, she found DeeAnn Martin's last email, and looked at her signature line for a phone number. She reached for her landline and punched in the numbers.

"Oh hey, DeeAnn, it's Cara Gerard. Do you have a moment to chat?"

"Um sure. What's up?"

Cara started with some real estate conversation. She'd only spoken to Hannah's assistant a handful of times and until the day after Hannah's murder, never about anything other than an appointment to show a property or the attendance at an open house. As she'd told Detective Driscoll, not a great many close friends in these offices. Cara wanted to ease into a conversation with DeeAnne about Hannah.

"Hope you are settling in over there. I bet Asako's a terrific manager. We were agents together in Williamsburg when that office first opened. She's smart."

"Yeah, it's fine."

"So—862 Carroll. Who's taking that listing? Under the circumstances, my buyers didn't actually get to see it, and we are definitely still interested." Cara wasn't sure this was exactly true, but knowing the Fishers, she could imagine a three-bedroom on Carroll Street for two million was one they wouldn't want to miss, murder or no murder. And Cara wanted to go in that front door again, for herself. She was thinking something might be triggered, and a clue of some kind would be jiggled out that would lead to something helpful.

"Well, I don't know, but Laura was talking to Patrick

about taking Hannah's listings. I figured Sally took us onto her team to get Hannah's listings, but she said she wouldn't drive all the way to Park Slope for less than three million. Although, Hannah had a lot of stuff pending and I bet Sally changes her tune. I'm pretty sure now, though, that Patrick wants to keep them in the Park Slope office. So anyway, ask him about Carroll Street."

"Will do. Gosh, it'll be weird to go back in there for me. I don't think I'll ever get over seeing her like that." She paused for a response from DeeAnne, but nothing. "Is anyone else looking at it that you know of? Had anybody else made an appointment to see it that day?"

"No, just you. We had a good turnout when it was first launched, but showings had slowed down." *Well, that answers that question.*

"Have you talked to that Detective? I mean since the day after it happened?"

"Yeah, he asked me if I knew she'd been having an affair."

"And did you?"

"Not really. I mean she didn't discuss her personal life with me. But I knew she had more than one phone, so you know . . . I said something to her about it one time, and she didn't even respond. Just changed the subject pretty quick."

"Did you tell the police she had two phones?"

"Yeah. Well not the first time I talked to them. But later I did. Why?"

"Oh, I guess I was just thinking that maybe whoever did it was whoever she was having an affair with. And maybe it would be as easy as that."

"Why would someone she was sleeping with want to kill her? That's pretty creepy."

"I don't know. You're right. Probably not."

"And it seems to me that if her husband knew she was sleeping with someone else, he'd want to kill that guy, not Hannah. Though that Detective asked me about him."

"Did they seem to have a good relationship?"

"I guess. I didn't see them a lot. But I didn't hang out with Hannah outside the office."

"Hmm. Well, I'll talk to Patrick about Carroll. Good luck with Sally. Maybe we'll do a deal together soon. I have a listing coming up in Williamsburg. By the water. I'll send you info when it goes up." She said her goodbyes and hung up.

Two phones. There's a way to have a secret life.

Laura's desk was the last one on the long row by the windows, and she sat facing away from the side street. Her row was the closest to the desk formerly known as Hannah's. Not the same view at all, but proximity to her BFF was most likely the reason for her location. When she had joined Corbin-Wheeler it had been at the suggestion of Hannah, was the way Cara had heard it, and Laura must have seen the advantage right away of sitting within chair-scooting distance of her more experienced friend. She had stayed put, even when they renovated the office, and she could have snagged a better view. It certainly made sense to be in a position to easily reach out to Hannah for input.

The office upstairs was mostly empty, as Laura sat

studying her computer screen, right hand resting on her mouse. Real estate these days meant a lot of time online. Cara walked over from her own desk in the back where she shared the area with Jim and Tom and another long time agent, Tracey McCloud, and sat down in the available chair next to Laura's. "Hey, how's it going today?"

Laura looked up from her screen. 'It's awful, is how it's going. I'm, like, a wreck?" Cara could see that Laura didn't look her best. Her eyes were puffy and red, and though it was apparent that Laura had tried to cover it all with makeup, it wasn't camouflaging the fact that she'd been crying. "I've been arguing with Robbie for days, and I can't sleep? I don't know how I'm supposed to, like, work."

Cara nodded. "Can you just stay home for a couple of days and rest? What will fall apart if you are not here?"

"How about everything? I don't want to stay home, anyway. I wouldn't mind going to, like, Cabo, but otherwise, I have too much work to do to stay home. And Patrick wants me to take some of Hannah's listings, right? So you know . . ." Her voice trailed off and she sighed.

"Well, she was your best friend. It's gotta be hard." Cara wondered what Laura and her husband were at odds about. "Why are you arguing with Robbie?"

"Oh I can't shut up about their affair. It would have been better for me if I hadn't found out right before she was killed. If I'd had some time, you know, to like, process? I'm not supposed to be mad at her, but I am! And now she's dead? Rob says it happened a long time ago and I should just get over it. He says I sound like a crazy person—and I guess I do."

Cara paused. *Ahh. There's a life partner who could use a little relationship training. Rob cheats on his wife with her best friend, and then accuses her of being crazy for letting it affect her.* "Well, it is confusing. I can see that. Your best friend disappoints you and you've got no opportunity to work through your feelings." Laura nodded and sniffed. "Maybe it would be good to talk to a professional. Maybe it would help you and Rob. Just a thought."

"Maybe. Rob would never do that though. He's like" (she put on a deeper gruff voice to mimic her husband) 'that's a total waste of money'."

"Sometimes I've had to try things that I didn't believe would help me. And oftentimes they do. I'm just sayin' . . ." Years of being in AA had taught her that. But Cara knew that most people don't ask for help until they're desperate. And even then it's sometimes more than they can do. Really she felt lucky that she was an alcoholic. It was more than a support group. She'd gotten through a great many hard things in sobriety with the help of its principles and other sober people. Things she might have tried to drink through, otherwise.

Cara stood to go. "If I can help in any way, let me know." She was pretty sure Laura couldn't have killed Hannah. And besides, she'd had an alibi. Shopping. But was it true that Rob and Hannah had no longer been sneaking around? What about those cell phones? Cara was pretty sure that it was not Laura's dark-haired, pudgy husband underneath Hannah on that fateful day, and she wanted to find out who it was. Any further inquiry, however, would have to wait. She had work to do, and these apartments wouldn't sell themselves.

Fort Greene, by Phone

Back at her desk, Cara scrolled through her emails to catch up on her buyers' responses and what they might or might not want to see. There were quite a few buyers that she was currently working with. And she had sent several new listings over to the Fishers and had asked them if they were still interested in seeing 862 Carroll Street. Finding a lengthy missive from Molly Fisher, with a detailed analysis of two of the new ones, and why they were interesting, Cara also read Molly's answer regarding the Carroll Street question. It was a decidedly positive, "yes!" *Well, good*, Cara thought. *I get to see it again, after all.*

Cara wasn't sure what she thought she would see, but she wanted the opportunity to revisit—more slowly and hopefully with a clearer head—the location where Hannah had taken her last breath. Both of the two times that she'd been there that day she'd been caught totally off-guard, and that was certainly the understatement of the year. Her heart had been racing, and in both instances she had been falling all over herself to get out quickly. Cara didn't think there would be anything there that the police hadn't found, but she wanted the opportunity to look around. She sent an email to Patrick, inquiring who had the listing, and when she'd be able to show it. And another one to Charlie Benton, asking about his Prospect Heights listing. Molly Fisher had expressed mild interest in branching out, and his three-bedroom on Sterling Place was one that might fit the bill. At any rate, Cara would use it as an excuse to have a conversation with him. She wanted to get a feel for Charlie's possible involvement with Hannah. He had a motive, after all, according to Dee Anne, and as Mary had pointed out, a bruised ego was reason enough for deep hatred. Would he have nursed his grudge toward Hannah long enough and deep enough to commit murder? Had an opportunity presented itself for Charlie to seek revenge?

Cara looked at his listing, formulated some pertinent questions, and picked up her phone. While she waited for him to answer, she thought back to that last text she'd received from Hannah: enthusiastic and totally unaware of the danger she was putting herself in. One minute full of piss and vinegar, as Pop Wesson would have said—and then gone the next. *Life is a mystery.*

Charlie Benton answered his phone with a tone of voice that sounded much like the way he looked, moving through the world: Full of swagger, verging on arrogance. "Hello, it's Charlie. How can I help?" *Oh brother.*

"Hi, Charlie. Cara Gerard here. How are you?"

"Well, Cara, I'm fine, how are you? I saw you at Hannah's memorial service the other day, but I had to rush to an appointment and didn't get a chance to say hello." Cara had been wondering how to bring up Hannah, but now she didn't have to worry. Charlie did it for her.

"I'm fine, thanks. Yes, I saw you, too. It was certainly a big turnout for Hannah."

"Well, it was. I heard you found her. That must have been a jolt! But you know, not to speak ill of the dead, she probably was one of the more disliked agents in the biz, don't you think? I mean, come on! You've been around. Did you like her? She was really successful, I'll give her that, but she could piss people off! And she didn't seem to care. I bet if people were honest, there'd be quite a list of agents who aren't sorry to see her gone."

Cara grimaced. *Tell me how you really feel*, she thought. "Well, she was always sure of herself, I'll give you that. But pissing someone off bad enough that they'd kill you for it? That's a whole different level of anger, wouldn't you say?"

"I suppose. But if anyone could do it, it would be Hannah. I don't think there was much she wouldn't do to get her way—to make a deal, or get ahead. And that's something I experienced first hand. I'm glad I wasn't in town last week, or I bet I'd be on the short list of suspects, myself. She and I clashed on more than one occasion. She was a liar and a cutthroat. There—I said it. No love lost between us."

Cara was surprised at Charlie's candor. He seemed to be completely unaware that his statements might indeed put the spotlight on him. "You were away? Lucky you. Fun or profit?" Cara wanted to know why he felt so free to express himself in this way to her. After all, it was common knowledge that he and Hannah weren't on good terms, but this was certainly up a notch or two from that.

"Oh, I was upstate skiing. Left Friday morning. Was on the slopes at Hunter in the afternoon. I didn't hear about it 'til Saturday. But let me say this. I felt sorry for her family, but it didn't wreck my weekend. I know that sounds harsh. But I'm not going to go around pretending, just because she's dead. Obviously, I am not the only person she stabbed in the back. I wasn't the first, and again, obviously, I wasn't the last. I had a visit from a police detective, and I said basically the same thing." He chuckled, bitterly. "Yeah, I'm glad I had that lift ticket still in the pocket of my parka!"

"Yeah. I hear you." Cara was ready to be done with this conversation. The toxicity here was upsetting, to say the least. And apparently Charlie had an alibi, though she wondered if he really had the lift ticket from Friday. "How's your listing on Sterling Place? Is it still available?"

"No, contracts are out, and it's looking pretty solid. Why—got a buyer?"

"Possibly. Let me know if there's a glitch. Or if you get another three-bedroom that looks that good. My people are really Park Slope, but they would consider Prospect Heights or Fort Greene." She said goodbye and hung up. It was lunch time and Cara realized she was hungry. She reached into the drawer that held the menus from the neighborhood eateries, and ordered a salad to be delivered from La Bagel Delight.

Well, I guess I'll check ol' Charlie off the list. Skiing, huh? Detective Driscoll had apparently taken her suggestion that Charlie had had a motive, and spoken to him. And most likely had checked out his alibi. Cara chuckled to herself. *Alibi. Motive. Ooh, Cara. You sound like a regular Miss Marple!*

7th Avenue and Berkeley

Okay, I've had enough. Cara finished up her searches for various clients, then closed out her computer. She folded up the empty to-go containers from lunch into their bag, straightened up her desk, and reached for her jacket. Throwing her big leather satchel over her shoulder, she started for the stairs. As she rounded the corner, Patrick intercepted her.

"Oh, hey. I was just coming up to talk to you. You got a minute or two?"

"Come on back. Let's sit at my desk."

Patrick followed her back, sat and moved Jim's desk chair closer to Cara's to sit. "How're you doing?"

"I'm okay. Trying to stay on task. I must say, I'm a bit

distracted. Hard to get Hannah's death out of my mind. But mostly okay. How about you?"

"Same. And I don't have the image in my brain that you do. Still, so disturbing. I am going to have a person from HR come speak to everyone this week about safety on the job. What people can do to protect themselves on showings and such. I don't know what new can be said, but a reminder of protocol can't hurt."

"That's smart. I get the feeling that it was someone Hannah knew, but you never know. And you're right. Most of us are complacent when it comes to that sort of thing. You haven't heard anything from the police, have you? It's been almost a week. I was hoping they'd have found whoever did this, by now."

"No. I called that detective—Detective Driscoll—this morning, but he said they're 'working some leads'. Whatever that means. Gosh, I hope it's not anyone *we* know. They've interviewed just about everyone in the office. I hope they get it wrapped up soon."

"Me, too, Patrick. Hey, by the way, who's got Hannah's listing on Carroll Street now? My buyers still want to see it, unbelievably enough. They didn't get in to see it, of course. Is it available to show?"

"Yeah. I have the keys. I haven't assigned it to anyone yet, but you can go in. Driscoll let me know this morning that they were through with their . . . whatever. It will need to be cleaned, since they dusted for fingerprints, so I arranged for that. It'll be good-to-go after 2:00 tomorrow.

I'll leave the keys at the front desk downstairs. You can just take them and bring them back when you are done."

"Terrific. Thanks. How weird would that be, if I sold it?"

"Right? Well, I hope you do, Cara. I really do." Patrick stood and pushed Jim's chair back into its place. "Something good should come out of this. Especially for you. That must have been a terrible thing to see."

Cara left the office and started for home. Thinking about her list of suspects, she reached into her pocket, grabbed her phone and called Mary. The voicemail message answered, and Cara waited for the beep. "Hey, let's eat somewhere good. We've got a murder to solve. And I have some interesting updates."

Cara unlocked the door to her apartment, stepped inside, unzipped her short Frye booties, and traded them for sheepskin mules. *Ahh. Tea time.*

When the water boiled, she poured it over the Harney and Sons sachet in her cup. Cara knew her mother would have been mortified to see tea prepared like that—instead of in a proper pot—but Cara preferred it this way. One bag, one cup. Victorian London Fog was a variety of Earl Grey that she and Mary had discovered and declared the absolute best of blends. It was buttery and smooth, very rich. Mary said it was like candy. Cara now ordered it in bulk, and she and Mary often split a jumbo order, to assure themselves that they never had to drink a lesser variant. Cara even carried a small container in her purse at all times with a few bags in it so that when they ate out, there would always be a perfect finish to their meal. They laughed about their obsession, but it was one that Cara didn't fight. There was no twelve-step meeting that she knew of for addiction to tea. Mary called just as she sat down and they decided on the Santa Fe Grill on 7th Ave. The two went there intermittently, when they were feeling sheepish about the frequency of their visits to the Club, or had a yen for fish. They both always ordered the same thing there, as well, and were staff favorites.

Mary arrived first, and was sitting on the metal bench outside the restaurant as Cara strolled up.

"Am I late?"

"Nope. Right on time. Just like always. How was real estate?"

"Pretty good. The Fishers still want to buy an apartment. And they even still want to see the one on Carroll!"

"Tenacious, those Fishers! Speaking of which—what's happening on that front? Any news from that detective?"

"No. But I have done a bit of sleuthing on my own."

"Do tell."

"Well, before I get to that, here's a weird, though tangentially related, story." They sat and when the waitress arrived, they waved off the menu and both ordered the fish tacos. The young woman nodded and poured water into glasses and left the pitcher on the table. Cara told Mary about Hayden and the shiva—and about her lunch with Lynette. She wanted Mary's take on it all.

Mary listened without interrupting, and then sat back,

looking thoughtfully at her friend. "Are you thinking this woman had something to do the murder?"

"I don't know what to think. My brain is working overtime here."

"Maybe she was upset about her son and Hannah having an affair, if it was him. Or maybe Hannah got greedy about their arrangement. Could she have strangled Hannah all by herself? Maybe she and what was his name—Hayden?—killed her together. I don't want to denigrate your standing as a realtor, but it does seem odd for her to come up with this plan, having just met you. But why not? I bet she reached out to what's his name—Syd—to find out about you."

"I'm not certain how to interpret Lynette Carlisle's attention either. However, I'm pretty sure I'm going to go with it, at least until I find a reason not to. And maybe another meet-up with her will enable me to find out more about that son of hers. See if I can figure out if he was Hannah's afternoon delight." She shook her head. "If so, I'm bewildered as to whether he killed her or not. Why would he?"

The two friends paused in conversation as the waitress delivered their plates of food. Flakey salmon, avocado, lettuce, tomato and cheese in a soft corn tortilla, done well, was a combination of flavors that was hard to beat. Cara was particular about Mexican food, because she felt she had eaten the best in her years in Texas and New Mexico. The two areas offered up vastly different styles, of course, but Cara appreciated this New York attempt at getting Northern New Mexican cuisine right. She'd been surprised to find this restaurant when she came to Brooklyn. It wasn't exactly Santa Fe—they didn't have Hatch green chili, for instance—but it was good.

Cara also brought Mary up to speed about Charlie Benton and his animosity for Hannah. "Apparently Detective Driscoll followed up after I mentioned him. Though I bet his name came up from other agents during their interviews. He wasn't at all tight-lipped about his dislike for her. I'm sure I wasn't the only one who ratted him out."

"Anyone else from your original list that still seems plausible?"

"Well, I don't think Laura Simonson or those two assistants are still on it, based on conversations I've had with them. I really haven't gotten to speak with Ben Bauer except that one time since the shiva, but my gut says he didn't have it in him. Maybe Hannah's killer was random."

"Well, motive, means and opportunity. That's what "Murder Plots 101" would say. At least that's what I learned when I wrote for *Billy's Daughter*. This doesn't feel random to me, does it to you?"

Cara shook her head. "Nope. It doesn't."

"Well, pay attention. Keep me in the loop and be alert. You know what they say—'the world needs more 'lerts.'"

The Office

Saturday morning was cold and overcast, but Cara's weather app said it was supposed to clear up in the afternoon. She was hoping that to be true, since she had confirmed a late afternoon time for showing Molly and Dan 862 Carroll Street again. It would be terrific if they could have a really good experience there this time around. Cara moved through her rituals early this morning, with coffee and meditation, before she got ready to go to the office. Lynette had texted "yes" for meeting at 11:00, and there were some show sheets with property info to print up for Sunday's open houses as well. Tom and Jim were launching a new listing in Windsor Terrace and she had promised to run by with a couple of rugs they were borrowing, to add to their staging efforts, before driving to the office. They were getting a lovely one-bedroom apartment ready for a Monday photo shoot. The friends often loaned furniture or finishing touches to each other's listings. It was nice to exchange pieces so that the photos always looked fresh. And Cara and Mary had theater tickets for an eight o'clock curtain from their subscription series at the Theater For A New Audience. They would be walking over together after Cara's showing with the Fishers, since this theater was in Downtown Brooklyn. All in all, an easy and pleasant Saturday.

She was planning to stop at Cousin John's Bakery on 7th to pick up some croissants on her way. She would offer Lynette a little nosh. Cara wondered if she could turn the conversation with Lynette toward Hayden and Hannah. She smiled to herself. *Ply her with pastries.* She really wanted to know if Hayden could be that guy with Hannah on the rug, or merely a business associate. Being direct with Lynette was one thing, but exposing her suspicions of the woman's son and his personal life was quite another. Especially if it might involve murder!

She wrestled the rugs from her storage unit in the basement of her building into her car and headed over to Windsor Terrace, the neighborhood just to the south of Park Slope. It was lovely, and mostly still old-school Brooklyn. The two neighborhoods met right at the south end of Prospect Park, the 585-acre design by Olmstead and Vaux—the same team who, in the mid-1800s had created Central Park across the river in Manhattan. Brooklynites liked to say that the duo corrected all the mistakes they'd made in Central Park. Brooklyn's Prospect Park introduced the term "landscape architecture" to the English language, and the park had been and still was a huge draw to the area. It was always full of families and joggers and dog-walkers even in February—and this Saturday was no exception. Cara drove up Prospect Park West carefully, aware of the foot traffic, and mindful of cars double parked to unload kids.

The co-op Tom and Jim were staging was a third floor walk-up, in a red brick townhouse, on tree-lined 16th Street, just up from Terrace Bagels. There was a line out the door and down the block at this borough's most well-known bagel shop. Nobody minded waiting for the fresh, warm neighborhood staple here. It would be worth the wait, she knew from experience. But not today. Cousin John's fare was a bit more varied and little more upscale, which was just what Cara wanted to offer Lynette.

She texted Jim to meet her downstairs so that she wouldn't have to park her car, and then double parked to wait. Seconds later, both of her friends came out to the street, and she jumped out to open the hatch and help them with the rugs. "We got it, Cara. A million thanks! Want to come up and see the apartment? It's so cute!" Jim hoisted the larger rug onto his shoulder and started toward the door.

"Oh, not this morning, y'all. Can I come Monday during the photo shoot? I'm meeting Lynette Carlisle at eleven at the office this morning."

Jim paused while Tom dug in his pocket for the key, and turned to Cara. "I heard about that offer, honey! That's fabulous!"

"Yeah, we'll see. It could be good! But I also want to find out if there was anything between her son and Hannah." Cara waved and jumped back in her car. "Let me know if you need anything else. I got some new wall art for that last townhouse and it's currently not in use. Neutral greys and browns."

"Will do, and thanks again."

Turning at the Park, she made her way back to Park Slope, parked on Union Street, and walked the block to the bakery. She had just enough time to pick up those croissants and then come back and print show sheets for tomorrow's open houses. Cara wanted to also take a minute or two to gather her thoughts, for her conversation with Lynette. A careful approach was warranted for this meeting on all fronts.

At a minute before the hour, the weekend receptionist buzzed the phone on her desk. Cara picked it up. "Hi!"

"Lynette Carlisle is here to see you, Cara."

"Thanks, Jill. Will you show her to the conference room, and tell her I'll be right there?" Cara grabbed the referral agreements that she'd gotten from Patrick, along with the box from Cousin John's, and headed to the big room near the front of the office that served as a space for agents to meet clients, or small groups to get together. She greeted Lynette and turned on the overhead lighting. "Good morning!"

Lynette looked up as she took off her coat and offered up a small, tight smile.

"Good morning."

"I brought croissants, and can offer you a latte or cappuccino. We have a Nespresso machine! Would that be good?"

"I'll have a latte, if you're making one for yourself. Things have certainly become more elevated around here. We barely had a Mr. Coffee, when I was here last."

Cara thought Lynette looked a bit drawn this morning, or maybe tired. She seemed more than a little uncomfortable. "Have a seat, Lynette. I'll be right back."

Cara poured milk into the electric frother, popped a pod into the machine and pressed the start buttons. Minutes later she was setting the steaming mugs down, and scooting the box of croissants, along with napkins, down to the end of the table where Lynette sat. "Well, it's not Starbucks, but it's pretty good!" Cara offered the croissants and hoped that Lynette would feel comfortable enough to discuss Hannah and/or Hayden. The older woman sipped her coffee, and waited for Cara to open the conversation. "I really appreciate your thinking of me regarding the proposition we spoke about the other day. It sounds like an offer I would love to take you up on. I spoke with Patrick and he suggested we formalize it a bit, and sent over this referral agreement. If this looks okay to you, we can both sign off on it, and I'll look forward to working with you, Lynette."

Lynette glanced at the form, and reached for a pen from a glass container on the table. She signed it quickly, and slid it back to Cara. Cara signed and turned to the copy machine, and inserted the sheet of paper. Handing the original to Lynette, she sat down.

"How are you doing, Lynette? It occurs to me that Hannah was probably more than a business partner to you. You must be feeling the loss." Cara paused, and reached for a croissant.

"Well, yes. It's a lot to take in." The older woman broke off a piece of one of the pastries and chewed it slowly.

"When I met your son at the Bauer's he said that he and Hannah had done some work together over the years. I got the feeling they'd been friends, as well." Not exactly true, but close enough.

"Did he say that? I guess so. They were closer in age, and seemed to work well together. Business associates, though, really, I think, more than friends. Some of my clients hired Hayden to renovate their places, after she put their deals together and Hannah, of course, recommended him whenever there was a need. He is quite talented. He and his partner, Will, have been in business together ever since they got out of school."

"Oh, nice. Would I know his work? I mean, are there any recent projects in Park Slope that they worked on together? I'd love to see something he's done. Maybe I have and just didn't know it."

Lynette paused. "I'm not sure. I don't remember addresses, anymore, actually. Too many to recount." She finished the contents of her cup, and set it down. "Well, Cara, I think I'd best run. I have errands to see to, before I head back to Florida."

"When are you going back?"

Lynette stood and pulled her jacket on. "Oh, Monday,

I think, or Tuesday. Anyway, I will be in touch, whenever someone needs a connection. Thanks for the croissant and coffee."

She bustled out of the conference room, and headed for the door. Cara watched her go, disappointed. She'd been hoping for a bit more conversation regarding Hannah. It felt to her as though Lynette was leaving to avoid that. *Hmm. She's hard to read.* Cara picked up the cups, and started for the kitchen. She noticed beside the bakery box that Lynette had left the signed referral. *Oh, shoot! Oh, well. I'll scan it to her.*

Back at her desk, Cara started to gather her things. *Wait. I bet Hayden and his partner have a website. What's his name? William?* She reached into the side-pocket of her bag and pulled out a handful of business cards that had accumulated. *What did I do with it? Well, it was Carlisle and Croft.* She googled them, and opened up the website and began to read. *"Multidisciplinary architecture and design . . . specializes in residential . . . yada yada"' Nice photos. Bios . . . Masters program at Pratt, both of them . . . two decades of experience . . . Brownstones. Aha! Projects completed.* Cara scrolled through the numerous addresses. *Well, hello, Hayden! 862 Carroll Street! Why didn't Lynette tell me that? She must have remembered that address if it was a connection from Lynette to Hannah and Hayden. Maybe it didn't start with Lynette.* She opened up the MLS site, typed in the address, and searched under sold listings. Well, Hannah had been the buyer's agent eight years ago when it sold last. *Interesting. How can I find out if Lynette referred that to Hannah, or not?*

Cara moved her mouse to open another window, typed in Department of Buildings, and entered 862 Carroll Street. The dates for permits pulled from the city would be there, and she knew the tax records should have the owners' names. *There it is! Major renovation was completed just two years ago. Richard and Ramona Winston. Mailing address is in Palm Beach!* She jotted down the address, and thought for a minute. She went to the Real Estate Board of New York homepage, and looked up the mailing address for Lynette. Same apartment building as the Winstons! *Of course it's a Lynette referral! She knows them from Palm Beach—and probably Brooklyn, too. And Hayden did the reno. Probably connected by Lynette and Hannah. But what does that mean? Maybe nothing, except it sure feels weird. They all knew this house, is what it means, but so what?* Cara shook her head and glanced at her watch. If she left now, she could park the car and have some time in her apartment. *Grasping at straws, here?*

862 Carroll, Redux

Cara found a parking spot almost directly in front of her building. Nice! She pulled in, and gathered up her satchel. She had plenty of time for a cup of tea, and a slice of leftover quiche that she'd bought a couple of days ago from the Union Market, before she walked over to meet the Fishers at the Carroll Street apartment. Now that she was actually going back, Cara felt just the tiniest bit anxious. No doubt it would be strange, but not only did she want to see the crime scene again, she needed to find Molly and Dan Fisher their dream home!

She had just sat down with her tea and was reaching for her book of New York Times crosswords, when her phone rang. She saw who it was, and answered. "Hi Patrick. What's happening?"

"I just heard from the Fort Greene office. The police have arrested Charlie Benton!"

"What?!"

"Yeah, they picked him up at the office, and took him out in handcuffs."

"I thought he was skiing last weekend! I talked to him, and that's what he told me."

"Apparently his car was ticketed in the city on that afternoon, so he was not out of town as he'd said. And he checked into a hotel in mid-town at 5:00. That's really all I know, but I wanted you to know as soon as I heard."

Cara hung up and sipped her tea, thinking. *Charlie Benton!* She'd felt when she spoke to him that he'd given her a prepared story. Something had seemed off. Mary had nailed it. Ego and greed. She was looking forward to seeing her friend, so she could tell her she'd been right.

At 4:00, she scrunched the warm and slouchy grey beanie that her sister had crocheted for her for Christmas onto her head and wrapped the matching variegated scarf around her neck, grabbed her down parka, and zipped it on. The temperature was dropping as the sun moved lower in the sky, and she and Mary would be getting home fairly late. It would be cold. The ten minute walk to her showing felt good and Cara arrived to 862 Carroll Street with plenty of time to look at the "crime scene" before she put on some metaphorical rose-colored glasses, and see it as a dream home possibility. Turning the key in the lock, Cara took a breath and pushed open the door. She glanced thru the living room and toward the kitchen. She stepped into the entry and put down her bag. First things first, she began to turn on all the lights. The living room had high ceilings and plenty of original detail: beautiful crown moldings, waist-high wainscoting, an ornate mantel at the wood-burning fireplace, original pocket shutters. It was even lovelier than the photos. Light was still pouring in, even this late in the day. Though it was technically the first floor one entered, the lower floor was an English basement, with windows well above ground level, and gave the parlor floor elevation. The main living area was well above street level. Moving through the archway that separated the living room from the dining room, and into the kitchen, Cara made sure that every lamp was on to illuminate the space. This was a twenty-two-foot-wide brownstone, and she noted that one really felt the extra width. Most of the homes in Park Slope were eighteen or twenty feet wide—and some even sixteen—so the spaciousness of this one was felt immediately. While loads of the original detail was intact, it had been renovated in a really thoughtful and elegantly contemporary way. *Well done, Hayden.* Tall white cabinetry in the kitchen with simple white subway tile offered up a clean and minimalist backdrop for the modern, oversized, and high-end stainless steel appliances. It had a wall of floor-to-ceiling windows in the back, with huge sliding glass doors where the kitchen opened to the deck overlooking the yard. *Wow! This is good!*

She quickly went downstairs, turned on lights and glanced around. Cara's seasoned eye took in the layout, noted the laundry closet in the huge ensuite bath—as well as the two walk-in closets in the primary bedroom, organized and sparse, with garments all hanging neatly in the same direction—and peeked into the bathroom between the two smaller bedrooms. *This could work. Well, it could if the Fishers could forget that someone had been murdered in the kitchen.*

Walking back up the stairs, she slowed down and took in all the details of the upper floor. The kitchen where Hannah Bauer was killed didn't look like a dangerous place. It actually seemed comfortable and inviting, like a room where people could enjoy spending time. In addition to the cooking/prep area, there was space for a table and chairs—currently a round glass-topped metal table with four matching chairs.

Cara stood where the light pine floor of the dining room met the sparkling white tile of the kitchen and looked toward the front door. She pictured herself coming in that door just over a week ago, and seeing Hannah Bauer on the colorful rug in the dining room, noisily engaged in lively and boisterous sex, and then later, on the floor of the kitchen propped up against the lower cabinet, disheveled and lifeless and alone. Cara turned and looked all around, from the dining room through to the living room and around the kitchen to that glass wall leading out side. *That's a lot of glass.* She lifted her eyes to the narrow space where the glass met the ceiling, and saw it had been equipped with electronic shades. *Yep, you definitely needed those shades. Otherwise, people could see right in.*

The deck just outside the sliding doors was large and had a rectangular grey table with chairs and a covered grill on the right side and on the left, just in front of the stairs leading down to an obviously well-landscaped yard, a seating combo with a loveseat, two low-backed club chairs and a coffee table—all made of weather-resistant wicker. The tall magnolia tree in the back corner of the yard, though free of its leaves now, was probably gorgeous in the spring. Cara slid the doors open—*gosh, these are heavy!*—and stepped out to the deck. The oversized backyards on this block were separated by fencing from the neighbors on each side and from the adjacent backyards of the homes of the next street over. She glanced up and down the block and into the yards behind. These were very big yards, at twenty-two-feet-wide, and were extra long. She would guess at least sixty feet. As she turned to go back inside to wait for the Fishers, movement from the deck one house over, and with the yard facing this one, caught her eye. A woman, small and with spiky red hair was climbing the stairs toward the deck and appeared to be talking on a cell phone. Cara stopped in her tracks and frowned. Is that Lynette? Brows furrowed, her mind spinning, she realized that she was looking over into what must be Lynette's backyard! *That must be Lynette's house on Montgomery Place. Right! And the backyards practically face each other! Of course! Montgomery Place is just one street over from Carroll!* Cara smacked her open palm to her forehead. She hadn't thought of that before now. Montgomery Place was one-way, and only one block long, between Prospect Park West and 8th Avenue. It didn't intersect the main artery of 7th Avenue through Park Slope, so unless one were seeking an address on Montgomery Place, it wouldn't be traversed at all. Essentially like a cul-de-sac.

Cara thought it was a very strange coincidence. She turned and went back inside, shutting the huge sliders with some effort. The more she thought about it, the more sure she was that something wasn't right here. The proximity was too close to not have meaning. Could what was happening in the kitchen be viewed from Lynette's brownstone? Maybe someone from there witnessed Charlie Benton? She would call Driscoll after this showing.

Molly and Dan Fisher arrived right on time. When Cara opened the door, both Fishers were typing into their cell phones. They looked up at Cara and smiled. "Everything okay in there?" Dan asked. "Nothing happening that shouldn't be?"

Cara smiled back, and stepped aside, gesturing them in. "The coast is clear. All good. More than good, actually. It's lovely!" She handed them both show sheets and floorplans she'd brought with her. "Let's check it out."

Molly and Dan shed their outerwear and walked through the living room slowly, noting aloud the details: the picture-frame moulding, the rich wood floors, the difference the extra width made to the feel of the space, the light. They had seen a great many apartments in the more than two months they'd been looking for property with Cara. They had moved out of the realm of being easily impressed, but she could tell they were liking what they were seeing.

Walking through to the kitchen, Cara pointed out the Wolf range, and the extra-wide refrigerator, along with the two-drawer dishwasher. Molly liked that there was plenty of room for kids with homework at the kitchen table. Cara muscled the sliding doors open, and they all stepped out onto the deck, and looked down into the yard. "Nice. I like it that it's landscaped already. Neither one of us has time to plant. Looks like all you need is maintenance, and water. I think we could manage that!" Molly laughed. "Our current place has such a small balcony. This feels enormous!"

Cara waited for them to take it all in, and she looked again over to the deck where she'd seen Lynette. And then all the way up to the top floor. If the shades were up in this kitchen, there was no doubt that one could see whatever was happening from any floor of that brownstone. When they turned to go back inside, she followed, and moved the door back in place. "Electronic shades, here. Nice!" She picked up the remote from the counter and pressed the arrow down. They all paused to watch, and Cara found herself looking to the left, past the fence, and back to what she felt sure was Lynette's deck, as the shades lowered, quietly. She thought she could see a face in the French doors. *Is that Lynette?*

The rest of the house tour went smoothly. The oohs and ahhs were frequent and audible as the three moved through the rooms, downstairs, Cara pointing out the ample storage, and the French doors out to the yard from the primary bedroom. The small patio situated under the deck contained a small bistro table and chairs. One could imagine coffee for two outside during the warmer months.

As they headed upstairs, Cara talked about maintenance fees associated with the apartment, as well as the age and quality of the renovations. The Fishers seemed enthusiastic, but somewhat reserved. They bundled themselves back into their jackets, and promised to check in with Cara, after they had had a chance for discussion. She said good night, and began to retrace her steps through the apartment to turn off lights and make sure things were locked up. She texted *Mary, Leaving in 5. See you in 10.* As she moved through, she couldn't help but ponder all the things going on in her mind: Hannah's murder, and all the people who resented her, Charlie's arrest, Lynette and Hayden's connections to Hannah and this apartment, and calling Detective Driscoll. *I'll call him on my way to Mary's.* Cara and Mary liked to stop for a light bite to eat at the BAM Cafe before a performance at TFANA, just across the street. They'd have just enough time if she picked up the pace. She was looking forward to something enjoyable this evening—a much needed break for her brain.

She turned off lamps in the living room, but left the light in the foyer on, for her exit, flipped switches for the overhead in the dining room and living room, and remembered the under cabinet light switch by the sink. It was already getting dark outside. She made sure the sliding glass doors were secured, and headed downstairs to the bedrooms.

Bedside lamps in the front rooms, and overheads turned off, Cara noted a narrow strip of light in the hallway floor itself that glowed softly, connecting the bedrooms and the bottom of the stairs. She hadn't noticed it in the light of day. *Hmm. It must stay on all the time, or be on a timer. That's pretty fancy.* She started into the primary bedroom, when she realized the lights were already off in that room, though the bathroom vanity light shone brightly from under the door. *I don't remember turning these off. Maybe it's connected to the hallway switch.*

She was reaching for the knob when the door suddenly swung open and a tall, thin man in black pants and a black hoodie stepped out into the room. "I bet you think you've got it all figured out." Cara froze in her tracks. Though he was backlit, she still recognized him from his photograph on line. Her heart pounding, she remembered what Jim had said about Hayden's partner: "Good-looking in a George Clooney kind of way." *Yep*, she thought, *that's him.*

Cara looked up at Will Croft and said, "How did you get in here, and what are you talking about?"

Will Croft took a step toward Cara, and she saw he had a gun in his hand, and it was pointed at her. She wished she had kept her cell phone in her hand instead of in her hip pocket. She had an alarm app that she'd downloaded almost a year ago, but it wouldn't do her any good now. And besides, she'd have to open it and then swipe. She was pretty sure a bullet could beat her to the draw. All she could think was Pop saying, 'don't bring a knife to a gunfight' yet that essentially is what she'd done. She thought fast, and started talking.

"You're Will Croft, right? Hayden's partner? What's going on here?"

"I saw you on the deck. And I know you saw Lynette. I think you know what's going on here." He pointed to the bench at the end of the king-sized bed. "Sit down. I need to figure this out."

Cara sat down. "Will, I'm not sure why you are here, and with a gun, but this isn't necessary. I'm just here to show the apartment. We don't have to figure anything out. How did you get in here?"

"I climbed over the fence and came in that door. We've had the keys since we did the work here." He leaned back against the wall as though for support. "I think you know I killed Hannah. When I saw you squinting over at our house, I knew you knew. I tried to tell Hayden you were going to figure it all out, but he said no. I knew you weren't as much of a hick as you sound. And Lynette thought she could fix everything with her little plan to buy you off. Why couldn't you just mind your own business?" Cara thought, *A hick? my ass.*

"Why did you kill her? What happened?"

"I didn't mean to! I was supposed to be in Manhattan pitching a job, but they cancelled as I was on my way, and so I turned around and drove back to Brooklyn. I was circling the block, looking for parking, and I saw Hayden go in the front door here. I tried to call him, but he didn't answer, so I went home and got the binoculars and looked over here. And I saw them. In the kitchen. Hannah and Hayden. Getting it on up against the refrigerator! I knew he was seeing someone, but I couldn't believe it was that little bitch. So phony, and full of herself! My skin felt like it was on fire! I couldn't think what to do. I tried to call him again, but no answer, and I got madder and madder, and then I remembered we still had keys. I went out the back and climbed over the fence and came in this door. I could hear them laughing and she was squealing and I don't even remember going up the stairs, but the next thing I know, I'm looking at the two of them. On the floor. Hayden sees me and starts yelling at ME, 'what are you doing here' like I'm the one who's doing something wrong! I couldn't believe it, and then, in walks Rich—Rich Winston—and starts yelling at Hannah, calling her a slut, and saying how long have you been banging him? And what about us, you bitch? And is there anyone else you're getting it on with in my house? And she stood up, and said something like, "everybody just calm down." And my head just exploded, and, and I pushed her, hard, and she fell back into the kitchen, and I guess she hit her head on the counter, because she didn't get up. I was yelling and crying and I didn't even realize it, 'til Hayden grabbed me and shook me, and said 'look what you've done!'" Will took a breath. "I didn't mean to kill her!"

Cara shook her head trying to make sense of what he was saying. "But she'd been strangled. I saw her."

"Don't say another word, Will. Not another word!" Lynette stepped into the room from the hallway, and walked towards him. "You have messed this whole thing up again." She turned to Cara. "And I had a feeling you were going to stick your nose where it didn't belong, Cara. I saw you out on the deck this afternoon, and I just knew it. I tried to throw you a bone, didn't I, but somehow I knew you were going to muck this up."

"What do you mean, strangled?" Will turned to Lynette. "What does she mean?"

"It doesn't matter, Will. I told you I'd take care of it. Now put that gun down. I'll take care of it!"

Will took a step forward, and pointed the gun at Lynette. "What does she mean?"

Lynette looked at Cara, frowning, and blew out a big sigh. She turned back to Will. "Well, when Hayden called me at the house and said that Hannah'd had an accident"—she used the two fingers on each hand to make air quotes—"he knew I'd come and figure out what to do. I came over here and you and Hayden and Rich all panicking and shouting and not thinking at all. And you saying, I'm sorry, I'm sorry. And Hayden saying, you killed her! And Rich—standing there waiting for something, I don't know what! And then he said, I'm not supposed to be here, I can't be here! So I handled it, like I always do! I got you two out of there, and I told Rich he had to help me, and we started wiping everything down so there wouldn't be finger prints anywhere. We got towels out of the cabinet, and I was methodical. And we cleaned everything up, doorknobs and the refrigerator, and everything. My mind was racing and I was thinking okay, we will just leave it here. And I looked around to make sure we had gotten everywhere, and then I heard her moan. I looked down and Hannah wasn't dead. Her mouth was moving and she was trying to say something. For Pete's sake, you hadn't even killed her! I couldn't count on anything from you or Hayden, and I looked at Rich, and he said oh God, oh no. And then he stood up, and he took her scarf off the table, and finished what you started. And—and I watched him. And then I said make sure she's dead. And he nodded, and I picked up the towels, and said to Rich, Go back to Florida. Go back to your wife. Will, I couldn't let you *or* Hannah ruin Hayden's career. Ruin his life! I took care of it."

Will Croft stared in horror at Lynette. "I thought I'd killed her! You let me think I killed her! How could you do that? You knew it was an accident!"

"I had to, Will! You and Hayden couldn't get yourselves out of this!"

"But I didn't mean to kill her, and now you're telling me she wasn't dead! I've been in hell about this, Lynette! How could you let me think that I'd killed her?"

"I did it for Hayden! And for you! I thought she was dead, too! Nobody'd have believed it was an accident, Will. I did what I had to do! Now give me that gun."

Will glared at Lynette. "Sit down, Lynette." Lynette didn't move. He gestured to the bench where Cara sat. "I'm in charge now, and I have to think. Sit DOWN!" Cara could see the anger and confusion on Will's face. Anger, confusion, and maybe some relief. Even with the gun in his hand and pointed in her direction, she felt sorry for him. Lynette sat down next to her.

"Will," Cara said, "you need to tell the truth." She knew she was taking a chance, but she had to say something. "It's important for you. It won't make this all go away, but you are not a killer. Your part in this was an accident. We need to call the police."

Lynette turned to Cara. "Shut up, Cara! Will, don't listen to her. We can take care of this. There's no way it works out, otherwise. Let me take care of this. For you and Hayden. Go home."

Tears fell from his eyes, as he spoke. "Stop talking! I need to think!" He put both hands, shaking, on the gun, aimed at Lynette, and leaned back against the wall, sliding down 'til he was sitting on the floor.

Cara spoke up gently. "Will, I will talk to the police with you. They can sort out the truth here, if you tell it. Don't let Lynette's version of this story be the only one that gets told. You didn't kill Hannah!"

"Don't be a fool, Will. I can take care of Cara. Give me the gun!" She started up from the bench, reaching towards Will, and then the gun fired—the loudest sound Cara had ever heard exploded in her ears—and she was thrown back into the giant bed behind her, as Lynette spun halfway around and fell on top of her. At that moment, several police officers burst through the door, weapons drawn, shouting, "DROP THE GUN!" Cara knew there was shouting, but it sounded far away, her ears loudly ringing and she felt as though she couldn't breathe, almost as if she were under water.

She heard someone calling her name, and she opened her eyes as Lynette was being lifted off her, and she saw Detective Driscoll crouched on the floor, between the bed and the wall. A sharp, acrid smell was burning in her nose, the movement in the room seemed blurry and she moved her hand to her chest, where she felt wetness. She looked at her hand and saw it was blood, and she drew in a sharp breath, as he said again, "Cara? Don't move. I think you are okay. Be still. I don't think that blood is yours. It's okay." She blinked hard, the lights came on and then her focus got clear. People were moving fast all around her. She heard Lynette screaming from the floor on the other side of the bed, "You shot me! You stupid little shit! You could've killed me!" And as Cara turned and sat upright, she saw the officers handcuffing Will Croft and moving him out of the room. She turned back and looked at Detective Driscoll, and smiled. "So glad you came."

He smiled back at her. "Me, too. You okay?"

"Think so. It wasn't Charlie Benton. Did you know that? How did you know to come here?"

"I got a call from your friend Mary, who said you were late in meeting her and that you were never late, and she thought you were here. She said she'd have my job if anything happened to you. So I jumped in the car and called for backup. I could tell she was a serious woman!" He shook his head and smiled again. "She sounded like she would do more than that, so what could I do?"

Cara looked at her watch and stood up. "Oh gosh, I AM late! We have theater tickets! Shakespeare!"

Driscoll started to laugh. "Well, you might not make it. I'll need a statement from you, and I think we will do that down at the station."

"Is Lynette going to be all right? Was she hit?"

"It looks like it grazed her shoulder, and went into the wall above the bed. You were both lucky!"

"I'm not so sure Lynette's feeling lucky. It's kind of a complicated story, but the owner of this house is the one who killed Hannah Bauer, and Lynette helped him."

"I can't wait to hear this story, Cara, but right now, let's go tell your friend that you are okay. I want her to know that I can keep my job!"

Mary stood at the gate at the bottom of the stoop. She looked up worriedly and flew up the steps when she saw Cara. She hugged her hard and then leaned back and looked at Cara's face. "Oh lamb, Are you all right? I knew something was wrong when you didn't show up after fifteen minutes. I started feeling uneasy, and I debated coming over here myself, but then thought I'd better call in the cavalry. And right as I got here, I heard that shot, and I have been frantic! And then I saw them bring that woman out on a stretcher. These guys wouldn't tell me anything! Oh, good grief, I'm so glad to see you!" She started laughing, and hugged Cara again.

"Mary, you are my hero! There's no telling how that would have ended, if you hadn't shown up with these guys! I'm so glad to see you, too!" They walked down the stairs together. "I have to go down to the station to make a statement, but can we have dinner after? And oh—I'm sorry we are missing Lear!"

"Oh, I don't care a fig about that. But I promise you, they will reschedule our tickets. We've been members since they opened! I think we've both had enough drama for one night, don't you? Dinner sounds good, and if you feel up to it, I want to hear about all of this."

After making arrangements to meet Mary at the Club later, and hugging her one more time, Cara waited for Detective Driscoll, as he jogged over to her and ushered her to his car. He opened the door for her and as she climbed in, she asked, "What was Charlie Benton up to, with that skiing story?"

"Oh Cara, he was just cheating on his wife, and his story was all worked out. Nothing to do with Hannah Bauer—but it was already there, so he stuck with it, until we caught his parking ticket. He had to come clean, after that."

"And what about Robby Simonson? What was he doing with Ben Bauer? I thought I was on to something there."

"Well, funny you should ask! Robby was just arrested by the FBI, for insider trading. You'll see it in the papers in the morning. Ben and Hannah, both, were instrumental in bringing him down. They were working with the Feds, undercover. That's why Hannah had a second phone and was setting up meetings with him. She wasn't having an affair with him. At least, not currently."

"What?! Poor Laura. She was duped all the way around. Will her husband go to prison?"

"Undoubtedly. I talked to an agent I know at the Bureau who said that when they put him in handcuffs today, Laura was so happy because she heard that the second cell phone was used to commit a felony, instead of setting up illicit sexual trysts! She was laughing and kissing him all the way out the door!"

After giving her statement, Cara stepped out of the police station, and anticipating the cold, wrapped her scarf tighter around her neck. She texted Mary that she was on her way to the Club. Walking over, she thought about life and relationships and how much of a difference one day could make. How different things would have been if Will's appointment hadn't been cancelled, and he hadn't seen Hayden go in that door. Or if Hannah had known that Cara was showing the apartment on that Friday, maybe she wouldn't have met up with Hayden at all. Or—Cara shook her head and sighed. Lots of what-ifs.

There was a saying that she'd heard many times in her years in AA: that it often came down to seconds and inches—meaning that terrible things were sometimes avoided, or not avoided, by very narrow margins. Hannah's death seemed to be one of those terrible things. For Hannah, for Will and Hayden, and for Lynette. Bad choices made worse by fear, or greed, and careless decisions leading to actions that couldn't be undone. Cara knew, despite her own losses and the mistakes that she'd made in her life that had wreaked havoc, or at the very least changed its trajectory, she had been lucky, so far. She'd found recovery, and it woke her up, giving her a shot at redemption, and more than a few second chances. *Note to self: stay awake.*

Home

Cara opened her eyes and looked over at the clock on her nightstand. The sun was streaming in her window. Nine o'clock! She hadn't slept this late in years. *I guess it's exhausting to get shot at.* She got up and put the water on for coffee. She didn't have to be anywhere today 'til noon, so really, there was plenty of time. She opened her laptop to see if anyone had reached out to register for her open house. Oh, good, a couple of agents, letting her know that they'd be sending their buyers over. And there was an email from Molly and Dan, with 862 Carroll Street in the subject line. Cara blinked, opened it up, and started laughing. The Fishers wanted to put in an offer!

About Carol Graham

Born in Texas, Carol Graham currently lives and works as a realtor in New York City and the Hudson Valley. Before moving to Brooklyn, she did a variety of work—in the ski business, as a bartender, a massage therapist, a driver for hang glider pilots, a photographer, a film reviewer, and once even worked in a bullet factory. Her love for all things Brooklyn began the day she moved to the city from New Mexico more than twenty years ago and has only grown as she has gotten to know and appreciate the neighborhoods and the people who live there.

I want to thank my Woodstock writers' group who spurred me on, especially Terri Wagener. Also, Lynda and Jenn were smart and valuable proof readers and helped me so much, as well as my friends who read and offered support. Karen Richardson gave me patient guidance and shared her knowledge in all areas of book design, and most especially I'm grateful to Casey—who has always given me the benefit of the doubt, or at least acted like he did.

Find out about the next Brooklyn Murder Mystery

Terror! In Windsor Terrace

by visiting
BrooklynMurderMysteries.com

Made in the USA
Columbia, SC
01 February 2024